"I Could Easily Dismiss You If You Weren't So Honest With Me."

"I would never trick you," Bill replied.

"How about the saxophone tapes, last night in the car?" Tate countered.

He grinned wolfishly. "That's not cheating. That's being smart."

"How did you know I'm susceptible to saxophones?"

"You dance. Your body feels music, so you had to like saxophones. And if you don't get dressed right now, we're going to be very late getting to the office. I'll do the dishes unless...could you use some help with your shower?"

"There you go again, coming on too strong!"

"I'm only trying to be helpful, and you, with your dirty mind, keep putting a different meaning to my words."

She turned away, shaking her head as she walked to the bedroom—and closed the door behind her.

Dear Reader:

Welcome! You hold in your hand a Silhouette Desire—your ticket to a whole new world of reading pleasure.

A Silhouette Desire is a sensuous, contemporary romance about passions, problems and the ultimate power of love. It is about today's woman— intelligent, successful, giving—but it is also the story of a romance between two people who are strong enough to follow their own individual paths, yet strong enough to compromise, as well.

These books are written by, for and about every woman that you are—wife, mother, sister, lover, daughter, career woman. A Silhouette Desire heroine must face the same challenges, achieve the same successes, in her story as you do in your own life.

The Silhouette reader is not afraid to enjoy herself. She knows when to take things seriously and when to indulge in a fantasy world. With six books a month, Silhouette Desire strives to meet her many moods, but each book is always a compelling love story.

Make a commitment to romance—go wild with Silhouette Desire!

Best,

Isabel Swift
Senior Editor & Editorial Coordinator

LASS SMALL
Hide and Seek

Silhouette Desire

Published by Silhouette Books New York

America's Publisher of Contemporary Romance

SILHOUETTE BOOKS
300 East 42nd St., New York, N.Y. 10017

ISBN: 0-373-05453-X

First Silhouette Books printing October 1988

LASS SMALL

At the end of *Blindman's Bluff* (Desire #413), Bill's reaction to Logan, the hero, gave me another view of this villain. Along with Tate, I was curious as to why Bill had been at that fishing resort, so I got them together to see how it would go... between an ex-villian and my heroine.

To: All those who seek. May they find
compassion and give it.

One

As the woman was led to her table in the nicely crowded and elegant DeBoise's, Bill Sawyer saw that her serious gaze came to rest on him as if she knew him. For the briefest minute Bill thought she intended to come over to him. In some surprise, he laid his napkin on the table and prepared to rise from his chair. But she went on toward another part of the large, chandeliered room, and she neither hesitated nor looked back.

A stunned Tate Lambert was thinking: Good gravy, that's Bill Sawyer! Had he recognized her? Surely not.

Bill knew the woman had really looked at him. It hadn't been just a woman's evaluation or flirting but a real look. Had she thought that she knew him? She moved on across the room, and he saw that other heads turned so that eyes could monitor her.

In an evaluating study of his own, Bill decided that while she wasn't a spectacular woman, she was certainly outstanding. She was a tall brunette with a short, swinging haircut, and she walked with confidence, as if she had an inner knowledge and acceptance of herself. So his first reaction to her was envy.

He continued to watch, curious to see what man she met. And he felt another kind of envy, this time for the man whose companion she would be. That confounded Bill, for he'd become quite cynical about the female gender—with good cause—and if he was envious of an unknown man over a glimpsed woman, he was really bad off.

While he might allow himself to be diverted occasionally by a woman, he had no urge to become seriously involved with another one.

He saw that she had been seated across the room, at a table where five women greeted her with welcoming smiles. In the sedate buzz of dinner conversations that pleasantly filled the room, he could discern their soft laughter and exclamations. The sounds were invitingly charming to his ears, and that exasperated him.

Tate was grateful that the maître d' had known which table was hers and that her inane murmurs to her friends were covered by their greetings. Bill Sawyer! Who would have believed she'd run into him again?

That very same Bill Sawyer was considering the three empty chairs at his own table and feeling sour. He really didn't have any friends left. Well, that wasn't at all true. He could fill those chairs any number of times with congenial people. However, as he considered each of those people—in groups or singly—he knew there wasn't one he wished were there with him at that moment.

This restlessness had been riding him now for almost two years. There was no cure. He'd tried. If he'd been a pioneer, he would probably have pulled up stakes and moved on west, across the country.

He had tried more modern variations of that. He'd relinquished some of his responsibilities; he'd traveled, partied. He'd done about everything to find something new or different, to indulge himself, to be distracted. The only trouble was, he didn't know what he was trying to change.

How does a really successful man find a challenge? Especially a man who already has more money than he could ever use in ten lifetimes? So he'd set up a foundation and funded projects. He believed that right now the greatest nonhealth crisis in this country, besides the national debt, was illiteracy.

He knew that most public libraries had classes for teaching any person who wanted to learn to read. It was something he could volunteer to do, but teaching was a slow job, a job for patient, dedicated people. He didn't fit that category. Fortunately there were those who wanted to help; he just helped by supplying some of the money.

So there he was, Bill Sawyer, six feet tall, in excellent health and thirty-eight years old. He was divorced from a woman who had wanted other men. He had a daughter who was a stranger. And he was restlessly bored with life. The embarrassing part was that he could *be* discontented. He thought of all the people in the world who had less than he.

Why couldn't he just count his blessings, as his grandmother told him? He did do that, but the reassurances were empty. His mind knew he should be grateful, but his spirit stayed flat.

His sister and two brothers led full, busy lives. They were baffled by his discontent. His mother had told him to go nurse the lepers, to find someone who needed help. His father had said he was in a midlife crisis a little early, but it wasn't too late to remedy it; he should find a good woman, get married again and have more kids.

So he'd looked. There were those who were impossible, and there were those who not only came high but generally were so involved with their own lives that they barely noticed him.

Did he want to be noticed? With all the work and money he put into being anonymous? Why would a man who preferred to be unrecognized want attention?

Curiosity had drawn his glance back to the woman's table across the room. Champagne had been served, and her five friends were drinking a toast to her. A celebration? He called the waiter over and asked what the women had ordered for their meal, then, with the wine steward's assistance, Bill selected two bottles of 1985 Piesporter Goldtröfchen Spätlese Reisling to be taken to her table with his business card.

Without actually seeming to do so, he watched with studied nonchalance as the wine was delivered with a flourish. Not *too* much flourish, just enough so that it appeared special. It was well done, Bill thought. His card was handed to her, and she took it with hesitant fingers and appeared to read it. She didn't look at him right away. That caught his attention. He was sure she'd recognized him from somewhere. There had been that brief— *But she didn't ask the waiter where he was sitting!* So she did know him? Then why didn't she look over and smile in recognition of his gift?

On the other side of the room, Tate was arguing with her guardian angel. She protested that she'd behaved all her life—except for that one weekend in Canada. Surely Bill hadn't remembered her. In Canada he hadn't paid that much attention to her. She sat there holding his card, in a quandary, and didn't want to turn her head to see if he was watching her.

Over at his own table, Bill studied his plate and wondered how long it had been since he'd last been discomforted. He glanced over at her, and she was watching him. They stared at each other quite seriously, then she smiled with a faint cynicism and nodded once in acknowledgment before she turned away dismissingly.

She did know him, Bill thought. She had to know him in order to have reacted as she had. Why was she negative about him?

He noted that while she wasn't particularly thrilled with his gift, the other women at the table laughed and were a little animated. They would glance around at him, lean toward her to question her and comment among themselves. They were quite open in their curiosity about him, but she shrugged. *Shrugged.* However, it wasn't a shrug of dismissal; it was one that implied he was no big deal. Now that amused him.

So she knew him. How? His meal was served, and he ate slowly and automatically, as he did when any problem presented itself. Some people paced, some agonized, some doodled. Bill went on with his life as if nothing were off kilter. He was a professional problem-solver. He solved everything: business problems, people conflicts, sensitive situations, missing airline luggage. No sweat. The only thing he couldn't solve was himself.

But now he could be distracted as he solved this woman and her animosity—no, that was too strong a word. Her...indifference to him. Who was she? Identify the problem, he told himself.

Throughout his meal, he mentally reviewed all the women he knew through friends, acquaintances and businesses, looking for this woman with her confident stance, good posture, and free-swinging stride. He began to believe he'd met her, seen her somewhere. Where?

Finally having exhausted all the business connections he had dealt with in the past two years, he went on to travel. A woman on a plane? At a resort? Resort! Fishing? There was the redhead in Canada. The young woman with the three-colored hair who'd flooded his consciousness with longing. The redhead who'd loved another— That was the place! There had been another woman at the resort. What was her name? She'd come there, laid eyes on Bill Sawyer and chosen him for herself. Mm-hmm. And he'd rejected her.

There'd been a woman with her in Canada. Bill looked over at her table and checked out the other five, but the woman who'd been at the lodge with her wasn't there. Just she. A brunette, middle thirties, interested. Why wasn't she interested in him now? With the wine, he'd allowed her the perfect opening. And he was well worth her trouble. But she'd snubbed him. He smiled at his plate, thinking, a good hunter knows when to appear indifferent. The chase intrigues any man.

Curiosity had become intrigue.

Up in Canada, just two months earlier, she'd given every indication that she found him attractive, but he'd been distracted by the young redhead and he'd ignored the woman's tentative advances. That had been just over two months ago. He hadn't been interested then. But times had changed. Why not now, in Chicago?

She must live in the Windy City, as all those women were obviously friends. What was her name? Something different. Something easy. One syllable. He looked at her, his eyes narrowed, knowing her name was in his memory.

She turned her head and returned his look. His smile was one of his nicest and most unthreatening. She didn't smile back. His broadened. He realized then that she was going to make him work. Good. It would entertain him.

Kate! That was her name: Kate. Short for Katherine, probably. Ahh. Unhurriedly he finished his meal and asked the waiter to delay his dessert, then he rose and made his way to her table. She appeared to feel his approach, for she became still. Was she bracing herself? Why?

Had he done anything to make her dislike him? He tried to recall any confrontation. He couldn't remember having done anything awkward or rude. He'd ignored her, but in his experience women recovered rapidly from being ignored.

He smiled and leaned down a little, saying to the rest of the ladies, "Good evening." They all smiled back, as he'd known they would. Kate didn't. She looked up at him. He turned his amused glance down to her. "Hello, Kate. Been fishing lately?"

Tate stiffened. So, she thought. He knew her. He'd remembered her from that lodge, where she'd been so foolishly, so desperately, so idiotically trying for anything to distract her from—

Bill's smile to Kate became smug. There. Mentioning the fishing had let her know he remembered her perfectly well. There'd been something about betting. She'd bet she would get the most fish, and she'd caught only one, just barely legal size, and—oh, yes—she'd wanted to have it stuffed!

Bill shared his nicely honed chuckle and inquired. "Did the taxidermist really stuff that fish?" He was jubilant he'd remembered that for an opening.

"Yes."

Bill thought that minimal reply wasn't encouraging. He turned to the table in general and five pairs of avid eyes. He used the women to get a response. "A celebration? A birthday?"

"No," one eagerly supplied. "We're celebrating Tate's—"

And he'd gotten the name wrong.

But Tate interrupted her friend to say, "It's just a get-together. How nice of you to send over the wine. Thank you." She dismissed him as if he were an intrusive waiter by then ignoring him.

Bill wasn't easily dismissed. "I believe it's the custom to dance with the man who supplies the wine."

Tate's friends laughed and agreed. She was impatient with them. If they'd been quiet, she could have gracefully finished the encounter with Bill Sawyer, but with them championing him, she would be forced to either be courteous or treat him rudely. That was a difficult choice.

With a practiced bullying that Bill managed to make appear only positive, he took Tate's hand as he put his other hand on the back of her chair to assist her in rising. He didn't leave it at that; he gave his wicked smile to the other ladies and said, "Decide among you who will be my next victim." They laughed as Tate rose, and Bill led her over to the tiny dance floor.

As they faced each other before they began, she said coolly, "I didn't want to dance."

He nodded as if he understood, and replied, "It'll help the digestion."

She groused, "I would doubt that seriously."

He thought it wasn't a very good beginning.

They danced in silence, and it pleased him that he had the ability to enjoy dancing. With four children to train, his mother had been one of many who had helped supervise the sessions, recruit new students and give financial support so that their offspring were taught dancing, social manners and polite conversation. The lessons had begun at age twelve and continued in increasingly advanced classes until age sixteen.

Bill recalled that it had been a grim thing for the boys, who had always numbered fewer than the girls. But those reluctant males—who'd had to be dragged to the classes twice monthly—had learned the basics of ballroom dancing. This was probably the fourth or fifth time in Bill's life that he was grateful to his mother for having seen to it that he could dance well.

As he'd known, Tate was superb. Naturally so. He knew she hadn't wanted to dance with him, but her body reacted to the music, and her feet obeyed his guidance. She made it a pleasure. With her as a partner, a man could be willing to deliberately go dancing. He looked down into her stiff face. She might not be willing to accept a date with him. "Did I do anything to offend you?"

"No."

"Are you just naturally grouchy?"

"Yes."

He laughed. "No. You were the life of the party at the resort."

"You didn't even remember my name."

He shook his head once quite ruefully. "That little redhead had me on my ear."

"The rest of us did notice."

"She and Logan are a good match. I was just jealous." At least he had her attention. He smiled. "I was too old for her."

"You're not that old."

"Up there in Canada, I felt like Methuselah."

Tate lectured him, "All your life, no matter what your age, you're older or younger than other people. I find it unsettling that most professional athletes are ten to fifteen years younger than I."

He agreed. "I know the feeling." She was being kind to him. The thought was encouraging.

She continued. "But then I look the other way, at my mother's generation, at my grandparents', and I know how young I am."

"I believe you came along tonight for a reason. I've been feeling my life was over."

"You made that obvious in Canada. You're very restless."

"And you're not?"

She shrugged. "I've adjusted. I've altered my goals and expectations."

"No more..." He'd been about to say something else, but then the music stopped, and they slowly parted. He smiled down at her and did his best dance-school thank-you bow. And darned if she didn't curtsy exactly as she had been taught. Then she actually smiled. He guessed: "Mrs. Harris's dancing class?"

She nodded. "Probably the Texas version."

"I suppose you enjoyed the monthly soirees." She would, he thought.

"Dreadful. The boys mostly hated it—I was taller than all but one boy, who was impossible—and they would saw my arm up and down and step on my toes. They had no grace, no rhythm, no joy in it. Most men can't dance worth a darn." Then she hastily amended, "You do very well. You must be Mrs. Harris's prize student." She said that as she turned to go back toward her table.

While he was disappointed she was leaving the dance floor, he didn't try to detain her. "I had some postgraduate help from a professional."

"Your mother did that for you?"

He shook his head. "By then I knew that if I could dance even halfway decently it would be a plus."

"You're really very good."

"Could we have an evening together? I'd like to take you dancing."

"I don't believe so."

"Just to keep me from getting rusty at it? I haven't danced since I broke my leg in Canada."

"How did you do that?" Curiosity forced her question.

"Foolishly. It's a long story. It's only a couple of weeks since I got out of the cast. Before I risked asking you to be my partner tonight, I recalled you were a good dancer."

"I'm surprised you remember."

She was back to being aloof, he realized. By that time they'd almost reached her table, and he found himself murmuring, "Don't be miffed by me. I've been through a bad time."

"Haven't we all." Tate wasn't impressed.

"Anything I can help you with? I'm a problem solver."

"Yeah. Sure."

"It's actually my profession. I'm a troubleshooter, time-and-motion studier, problem solver. Use me. Do you have a card? I'd like to see you again."

"I don't think so."

"As an acquaintance," he coaxed her. "We could have lunch."

In a negative way she commented, "I have your card. Perhaps I'll call you."

He knew she had no intention of doing anything of the sort. However, there were five women whom he'd already asked to dance, and he was a clever man.

Bill was aware that all five women really liked Tate. And they liked him. He could be very personable when he chose, and from the five in turn, he discovered all he needed to know: that Tate lived at a marina on Lake Michigan and that she was Women's Page editor for the weekly *People's Voice*. He really didn't need to know more than that, but he learned that she'd taken back her maiden name—Lambert—after her divorce. Her last name had been the simplest to find out. At their age, who hadn't been divorced?

Just two days later, Robert MacLean—publisher of the *People's Voice*—invited Tate to lunch. He told her they would be discussing a series about women in executive positions.

The newspaper was an established one that was gradually taking on the format of a weekly magazine. Their building was an old one up the Chicago River from the Tribune Tower, and Robbie had chosen to meet at a nearby small, familiar restaurant.

When Tate arrived, Robbie was already at the table, and he stood up at the sight of her. He was tall, lean and distinguished-looking. Tate knew she shouldn't have been surprised when she saw that also rising from a chair was . . . Bill Sawyer.

"My dear," Robbie said, welcoming Tate affectionately, "Bill says you are acquainted. That's nice. He has a good idea for a series that you'll find interesting. He says you met in Canada when you caught your fish."

Tate knew Bill had maneuvered her. "Yes," she replied to Robbie, but with her slight smile and single nod to Bill she acknowledged the fact that she had to crown Bill's king.

Very satisfied, Bill nodded pleasantly in return. He had her trapped. He hadn't had to really inconvenience himself or risk her ignoring him, his calls or any note or invitation. There were times like these when it paid to know people. Like his tapping his dad's acquaintance with Robbie MacLean.

After the three had been served, Robbie mentioned in a conversational way, "Just a couple of weeks ago Tate was snatched and held along with her friend Carter under mysterious circumstances. She says she had no idea why, but it was an interesting experience."

"Who held you?" Bill asked her.

"They were disguised." Tate deliberately gave him a full stare, as if she had no inkling of who the captors really were. Then she lowered her glance to her plate and selected another shrimp.

Something about Tate's manner made Bill *know* she knew who'd held her. She'd never told anyone. "There were no clues in speech or dress?"

"All disguised." Abruptly she changed the subject. "Who are the women you've lined up for the series?"

He considered her. She knew damned good and well he'd arranged this meeting in order to see her again, but it appeared that she had no intention of helping him out at all. Perhaps she didn't want to work with him. If she had known he was also Robbie's guest that noon for lunch, would she have found some reason not to be there? Would she have sent someone else in her place?

It didn't matter. Right now, for this time, he had her nailed. He assumed a businesslike air. "There are women in our organization who would be inspirations for any career-minded woman. We thought you might like to tap them for the encouragement they could give to other women. I'll have a list and help with the selection and scheduling. It'll be a pleasure to single them out for attention because they're fine people."

Tate thought his willingness was a little overdone. He was trying to say that he wasn't prejudiced against women, that he was openminded and accepting. That's the wool he was trying to pull over her eyes.

She knew Bill Sawyer. He was a dominant male. He employed women only because they tended to work harder and he therefore got more for his money. She tilted her head just a shade and stared at him, soberfaced. He must think this was her first time out of the house alone.

Aware of her animosity and reading her perfectly, Bill licked his lips to hide his amusement. He even had to bend his head down, put his curled hand against his mouth and cough a little so that he didn't actually laugh out loud. But he knew his eyes brimmed with his humor. He was going to enjoy this. And he felt the stirrings not only of attraction but of desire. She'd been ready to flirt with him in Canada, two months earlier—why not now?

Robbie asked Bill, "Did you watch her fish at all? She's given up more bait than you'd ever believe possible. She is dedicated, but all she does is feed the fish. I had her over in Scotland, on the water there, and there isn't any way in this world a fisherman can avoid catching something. But not Tate. I couldn't believe it. I would have given anything to've been in Canada and seen her when she finally caught one."

She declared, "I was completely calm."

Robbie snorted in a gentlemanly way. "You were probably stunned."

Bill volunteered, "There was another woman there who caught one bare-handed in the water."

Robbie nodded. "That would tend to distract attention from one only legal size and caught conventionally."

"You're rude to keep referring to my fish as 'only legal size,'" Tate chided Robbie.

He supplied, "If you'd put it on a regular-size plaque, it wouldn't have been so ridiculous."

Bill questioned, "What size is the plaque?"

Robbie rolled his eyes. "A sailfish would be comfortable on it."

Tate defended herself: "I couldn't diminish it by treating it like a small fish."

Bill laughed out loud. He wondered how much he'd have to work before she'd relax with him and treat him with the fond carelessness she used on Robbie. He glanced down her body. He wanted more than fond carelessness.

Robbie continued speaking to Bill. "Since you know her, you understand how strange she is; that's probably why her section in the *People's Voice* is so popular. Have you read her page? No? You'll have to see the files. One always wonders how her stories will turn out. It lends an irritating stress to our lives at the paper. She stimulates us."

"I'm completely normal," Tate said perversely.

"See?" Robbie's words nudged Bill's attention. "Just her saying that shows how amazingly tilted her thinking has become."

Tate suggested, "Why not put me on the political page?"

"And disrupt the country?" Robbie paused as if to assimilate the notion of such a disaster. "Why, Tate, politics isn't ready for you! You ought to know that. You would tell the truth. Think how unsettling that would be in the world of politics." He sipped his coffee before he suggested, "You could do a series on the wives of politicians."

"Goody." Tate's word was not sincere.

To Bill, Robbie sighed, much put-upon. "She really is very difficult. I almost married her mother, you know. I comfort my grief over losing the mother with the thought that at least I'm not Tate's father."

Bill grinned, watching Tate, and knew it was not a new comment to her. Obviously she and Robbie were lifelong friends. Bill would have to ask his father about Tate's mother. He found he was curious about

Tate. Why would such a woman go off into the wilds of Canada to a rustic fishing lodge?

She asked, "Do I get dessert?"

"A scoop of sherbet, and that's all." Robbie scowled.

She lifted her chin. "I want the almond tart."

He sighed and looked off as he considered, then he bargained, "I get half."

"A quarter. It isn't on your diet."

And seeing the ease between Tate and her boss, Bill realized that if she didn't want this series, and to work with him, she could refuse quite easily. But she hadn't yet declined. For some reason Bill's heart lifted. How could a heart lift? What nonsense. But he was going to have the excuse to see Tate and be around her. To know her. While she might be reluctant, even unwilling, now she wasn't going to avoid him completely. He smiled.

And quite disgruntled, Tate Lambert sat—waiting for her almond tart—thinking that here she was, where once she'd wanted to be, with an interested Bill Sawyer. Now she didn't want him. After that fluke of a time in Canada, she had thanked her stars that Bill hadn't been interested. He would never want anything but a brief affair, and an affair was something she didn't need. Not with Bill Sawyer.

She gave him a raking glance. He was a tall, strong, black-haired, hazel-eyed bulldozer. He could wreck her, just because he was bored and didn't know what to do with his time. Whom did she know that she could drag across her trail in order to distract him from her?

But all the way through her savoring three-quarters of the almond tart, she found that she couldn't think of any woman who would be suitable to use in distracting Bill away from her. Not one. She was going to have to deal with him by herself.

The idea of her having any dealings with Bill sent a remarkable wave of shivers through her body. She'd been interested in him the first time she'd laid eyes on him, up there in Canada. And he'd spurned her.

She'd gone to that resort deliberately to be distracted. Away off there in Canada, where no one would ever know her. She'd made a bold and deliberate play for him that had been unsuccessful. Now, here she was in a position for a flirtation that could be carried to any degree. And he was interested. But she was at a strong disadvantage. He had the wrong impression of her; he thought she was really the way she'd seemed that one weekend.

It was exactly like her mother had always said: Never write or do anything you wouldn't want printed on the front page of a newspaper.

She thought that being rejected ought to have cured this strange attraction, but obviously she was still susceptible to him. She would think her pride would help out, but just sitting there next to him, she was so conscious of his body. That he breathed. That he looked at her. That he was interested in her as a woman.

She glanced sideways at him and a flood of strange shivers curled through her stomach and caused prickles along her breasts and in her thighs. She was a fool to be tempted by this man. She should get out of this assignment. But she knew she wouldn't. She would go ahead with this, flirting with disaster.

What was she doing to herself? What was she getting into? She didn't know. But she was going to see.

Two

Although her instincts had urged her to refuse the assignment, Tate didn't decline doing the series on women in the Sawyer network of businesses. She knew if she really had the brainpower Mensa said she had, she would hand this assignment over to Ellen right now. But she brushed such logic aside. However, before her initial working meeting with Bill, Tate tapped the grapevine for information on Bill's background.

She learned a great deal about how marvelous all women found him—the perfect man. Then there were the lurid scandals implied about his ex-wife and Bill's retrieval of his daughter from the woman's custody. Several women sadly mentioned that he was soured on marriage or a commitment of any kind, but that he hadn't lost his interest in women. And there were a couple of friends who added, "Be careful of this one."

So Tate compromised. While she wouldn't give it up, she'd make short work of any contact with him. She almost recognized that it would be called playing with fire. But she ignored the feeling. She would be efficient. Impressing him even as she discarded him. She'd get the survey under her own control and eliminate any need for him to be around. That was the way to do it, all right.

Bill was cheerfully, helpfully, diligently involved. She sat across his desk from him and felt grim. He was being deliciously charming. She knew full well that he was not the hero type. He was a dangerous pirate who would capture her heart and leave her abandoned in port when he sailed away.

The two of them were working in his executive office in the carefully renovated Sawyer-family building near the Tribune Tower. Tate had been there since nine that morning, and they'd been served a light luncheon at eleven-thirty. He was helping her choose six women from his organization. The responsibilities of each woman had to be different, but all were women who were in charge.

Tate wondered why Bill bothered. Surely there was someone else who could do this screening job. Actually, Tate didn't need any help. All she had to do was read the personnel files.

He'd declined permission for her to take the information back to her own office at the newspaper. While she could understand that rather extreme protection for his staff, she didn't see why *he* needed to be the one who helped her.

Tate thought she and Bill were a lot like two cats—the circling, interested, carefully moving male and the crouched, reluctant, spitting female. Tate even felt like snarling in a low warning for him to keep his distance.

She was annoyed by him. How like a man to ignore a woman, dismiss her, then, when she was thoroughly rebuffed, to turn around and prick up his ears! Men were difficult and unfathomable. But what other alternative was there for women?

She thought, just look at him, sitting over there, going over that woman's file. He was a perfectly made male. His hair was tumbled, the victim of his restless hand. He probably knew just exactly how that made some woman's fingers long to smooth the dark, silken strands—or maybe rumple them a lot more. Tate clutched her fingers together to keep them from twitching.

He used his body so carelessly. He moved as if it had been made to serve *him.* He walked it around, unmindful of its grace, and he dropped into chairs with complete disregard. He was a poor guardian of that body. She could show him how to take care of it. And she looked on it possessively.

Her mesmerized stare slid down the planes of his face to his strong throat. His tie was loosened and his collar button undone. How intimate that small glimpse of his throat seemed. She looked over his wide shoulders and permitted her eyes their examination of his marvelous chest. How irritating that he was sitting at a desk, partly concealed. She looked at his square hands. His fingers were long and blunt. She thought about those hands as she watched them move.

Then, as he read, he tucked his lower lip between his teeth and bit into it as he frowned over something. She was fascinated. She thought about saving him the trouble and doing it herself.

He looked up at her, blinked as he caught her gaze, and smiled a little. "Finished?"

She wasn't *nearly* finished. "Not yet," she replied gravely. Then she tore her stare from him, but she wondered how he could know she had him naked on a bed and was leaning over him, nibbling on his lower lip. Wait. What was she supposed to be doing in order that she could be "finished"? The résumés. Of course.

In a perfectly ordinary way he sympathized. "It really is hard to choose. We have some remarkable women working for us." Relaxed, he grinned at her. "We could keep you busy for a year, doing interviews and articles."

She thought, a year of sharing time with him. She would perish. She knew perfectly well that propinquity might eventually lure them into a net, but for him it would only be a temporary fling. Just enough to ruin her for all other men and destroy her life. Unfortunately, he was only on the prowl. How could he be in that room, alone with her, and be able to read about other women? A little sour, she said, "Most of them are younger than I."

He nodded, absentmindedly pulling his lower lip between two of his fingers. "My grandfather was in World War Two, and he said the air force expanded so rapidly—at the beginning of the war—that there were colonels who were only twenty and twenty-one years old. That's the way business is now. Everything is expanding. Training is exceptional. The population glut of the baby boomers is past. And the new generation below thirty is riding a wave of opportunity."

"That might be a very good basis for this series," she speculated. "Not just women, but the new future."

"We Baby Boomers are supposed to be running things, and we are the overwhelming number in the business world, but there are still a whole lot of us who never bothered to become involved. There are a lot of remarkable talents that have been lost by the sixties it's-not-worth-it attitude.

"This new generation is more dedicated. They are also more subject to stress and uncertainty. CEOs have found that these young people need bolstering in confidence. They are the authority figures and must deal with many people who are older than they. We have seminars for them." He grinned to share the amazement of it all. "And that's another series that might interest you—about all the help available now to train new office managers to solve almost any problem."

He leaned that marvelous body back in his chair and stretched his arms up, then raked one unappreciating hand through his hair . . . as she let her gaze run down the additionally revealed view of him.

One hand gesturing, his mind was on what he was saying: "If today's office managers have to fire someone or deal with an inept person or an indiscreet office affair, personal stress—you name it—there's help. About the only thing that would really help the younger working parent isn't given enough attention, and that's child care."

Tate wasn't listening. She was mesmerized by the window's backlighting of his eyelashes on the far side of his face. She thought how fortunate it was that she'd brought along the tape recorder.

He looked at her, and for a brief minute he was silenced by her being there. But he couldn't just stare. He had to say something so that he had an excuse to look at her. When he spoke, he had her attention, and having it was a little heady.

He noted that she was listening to him with unthreatening calm. Generally she was poised to contradict him. What a contrary woman! And she was so sure. She was the one his organization should get to teach its young female executives how not to be intimidated by aggressive men.

He frowned at her. If she hadn't been born with that attitude, she must have learned aggression somewhere along the line. "Do you have brothers?" He saw that she was a little slow in accepting his words. Where had her thoughts been, if not on his words?

"Sorry. What did you say?"

"Do you have brothers?"

She shook her head. "I'm the eldest of five daughters."

He thought she must be naturally aggressive. She had four sisters. Girls weren't ordinarily so confident. She must have had those sisters organized and running around from birth. He tried to visualize a sort of Little Women group. Tate would be Jo, as played long ago by a young Katharine Hepburn. He'd seen the film recently on cable TV when he'd been laid up with his broken leg. He stretched that leg now. It was still sore. It had been a little early to dance with six women last week. He smiled. It had been worth it. He'd found out what he'd wanted to know, and there was Tate Lambert, sitting in that chair in the same room with him.

Tate was watching him and saw the smile. How like a dominant man to smile indulgently over a family of five daughters. Bill and her father would get along great. Come to think of it, Bill had a daughter. "As I recall, you have a daughter?"

"Yes."

"Does she live with you?"

"No. I finally managed to get custody. But since I'm gone so much, traveling, Jenny lives with my sister and her family."

"Do you get to see her?"

"Not often," he replied.

Sure. He could sit around here, needlessly sorting through résumés like a clerk, but he couldn't bother with seeing his own daughter. He was probably embarrassed by even *having* a daughter. Domesticity—or the dregs thereof—was something of a burden to a swinging, divorced man.

Again she discovered that he was speaking: "My daughter's quite a baseball player."

Tate asked, "How old is she?"

"An excruciatingly awkward twelve."

Tate continued to be negative as she decided he was ashamed of a gangly child— Ye gods, *children*! she remembered suddenly, and looked at her watch. "I must go." She gathered her papers, placed those she didn't need on his desk and picked up the tape recorder, shutting it off. "Thank you so much for your time. You must know that it really isn't necessary for you to be involved. I'm sure you have other things to do. Someone else could . . ."

He rose. It wasn't even three o'clock yet. He'd plotted to ease her into going to supper with him. "An appointment?'' Did she have an afternoon date? "You don't have a car; I can drop you.''

"Well, it really—''

He went on easily, "Our company always picks up and delivers our visitors.''

"I can just call a cab.''

Ruthlessly he flicked through his calendar. "I've nothing pressing. Let me drive you.'' He smiled carefully. If he wanted her to be interested in him, should he smile wolfishly or blandly? Should he encourage her, or should he wait and allow her the initial approach? Games. How long had it been since he'd wanted to play them? Or needed to? Had he already lost his opportunity with her? He'd get her in his car, and then they'd just see. "I'll take you down.''

"Down?'' She glanced up. There'd been something very risky about his wording. No, the words were all right. It was his tone. There'd been a purr to it.

"To the car,'' he replied, his face bland and unthreatening.

But she was still surprised when he took her arm and walked her from his suite of offices. He nodded to his secretary and instructed: "I probably won't call in. Let Mack handle anything that comes up.''

Tate could see the woman was startled. Bill must never walk out this way. But the secretary stretched her surprised mouth into a smile and said, "Yes, sir.''

Tate gave him a sideways glance and narrowed her eyes suspiciously. And her suspicions were confirmed. A very nice car was parked next to the elevator in the underground parking lot. Bill handed Tate into the car, then he walked around the hood and got into the driver's seat. Tate said, "Bill, this isn't at all necessary.''

He gave her a rather pleased look and replied smoothly, "Your series is going to be good PR for my companies."

"But it doesn't necessitate the chairman of the board driving me around."

"Oh, didn't you know? Robbie said I was to take care of you. I'm only following the letter of his instructions."

"Bosh!"

He laughed. "Bosh! No one says 'bosh' in this day and age." He was pleased with the teasing.

Sulkily, unteasing, she changed it to a sharp "Baloney."

"I'll accept baloney."

"Any more and you'd burst."

She realized that he loved her sassy retort, and he was still smiling over it as they exited onto the street. He drove well. While he was an aggressive driver, he wasn't foolish or belligerent. She grudgingly admitted to herself that he was skilled. She knew because she watched him. The way his head turned to keep track of the traffic around them. The way his hands moved. The way his knees bent and the material of his trousers shifted and revealed his muscular thigh.

Bill asked, "Where is your appointment?"

She thought he'd appeared reluctant to ask. Did he think she was going to do an exposé on someone? Probably. "The Chicago Public Library Cultural Center, just off Michigan on East Washington."

"Right. Research?"

"No. I'm doing some volunteer work for them. This is a part of the reading program. We're taping some books. I read aloud quite well."

"A novel?"

"I've taped two. Today I'm doing one for children. The readings are with specific books so that the kids can read along."

"That's nice of you. How did you get involved?"

She looked out her window. She didn't mean to be silent. She was fretful, trying to think of a way to respond. She said lamely, "I just did."

That made him avidly curious. "How long will this take us?"

"There's no need for you to stay. I can get home easily from there."

"I'm curious," he admitted.

"It'll take too long. Into the dinner hour. These are mostly volunteers, and they work the hours and days that they can."

"I'd like to watch."

"You should read," Tate told him. "Your voice is excellent. Can you read smoothly?"

"I've never noticed."

She explained, "They like a man's voice for little kids. For the most part, the kids hear only women's voices."

There was underground parking beneath the building, and they used one of the guest slots. Tate taped an audio read-along in one of the glass booths. When the tape was available, those who checked the book out could take the tape to one of the individual learning desks, fit the tape into the machine and listen as they turned the pages. When Tate's voice would ask them to say the words aloud, they would say them unself-consciously.

It all took three hours. Bill was fascinated. Tate forgot about him for most of the time, but occasionally she would look up, and skitters would go through her, because there he'd be, watching her. Alert. Not bored or restless. There might be more to Bill Sawyer than she'd ever dreamed.

Bill asked Tate to dinner. It was almost six. She really didn't have any excuse not to, and he'd devoted so much time to her that day that she hated to be rude and decline. She mentioned to her conscience that she didn't owe Bill Sawyer anything. He was getting excellent public-relations exposure from the articles. She needn't do anything personally. She really didn't have to eat with him or spend any extra time with him. She was tired. She wanted out of her heels and panty hose. She wanted to wash her face. She balanced all that with inviting him up to her apartment. She didn't want him there.

He said, "Why not go into the rest room here, get out of anything you don't want to wear, splash some water around to cool off a little, and we'll go up the shore to a beach I know and eat some sinfully delicious junk food."

How could she refuse?

He stopped on the Loop at a fast-food place that was already closing. Like many small eateries in a business district, this one closed with the exodus of the daytime people. Tate got out to run inside—still wearing her shoes—to buy the dregs of fried sandwiches, French fries, and soft drinks. Then she ordered two chocolate sundaes. The manager allowed her to stay inside the door until Bill's car came around the block for her. Bill paused at the curb, and she dashed out amid the impatiently honking horns and got into the car. They pulled away, went to Lake Shore Drive and turned north.

They bravely fought the pickles' deliciously insidious aroma, which quickly filled the car, then they began to sample. Tate fed Bill as they drove along. A French fry. A bite of pickle. A sip of Coke. To touch his lips with her fingertips made an amazing tickling feeling curl along deep inside her core, causing her to stare at him. He'd smile and glance sideways at her. His eyelashes fascinated her.

They drove on north for a long way that August night. The lights came on, the day closed down, and it was magic. She broke the sandwiches into bites and fed them to him. She and Bill were hungry, and the drive had been long. He had a tape of saxophone music, and she felt carefree in a rather abandoned way. Her shoes were off, and she rubbed her bare feet sensuously on the lush dark blue carpeting of his car. Stopped at a traffic light, they'd shed their suit jackets. He'd loosened and discarded his tie at another; then later he'd unbuttoned and folded back his shirt cuffs, and undone a couple of buttons on his shirt front.

Eventually they came to a security fence, where he stopped to identify himself to the guard before he drove on through to the lakefront beach. A private beach, it was maintained by those whose houses lined the shore. There was no moon. But the distant city's lights and the darkness of the vacant sweep of natural lakeshore were marvelous.

He eased the powerful car to a stop, shut off the motor and car lights, then turned to look at Tate. He'd known being there would be a treat for her. He thought of her as a woman who loved nature. "I don't have a fishing pole in the car."

"I'll forgive you."

He opened his car door, and the lake breeze came to them, but when she opened her door, the breeze went on through the car, tousling her hair. Bill was taking off his shoes and paused to look at her. Then he pulled off his socks and rolled up his pant legs. "I intend to wade."

She laughed. Such a delicious sound to his nerves. How could he have been so obtuse up in Canada? Maybe he'd needed to mature just a tad more. How could he have allowed such a woman to slip through his fingers without tasting her? How had he gotten this second chance with her? It scared him a little.

Barefoot, they met in front of his car, and she handed him his melted sundae. They drank the sloshing, thick, maltlike mess, and it was great! They licked around their mouths and grinned. After they put the containers back in the bag in the car, they walked to the water. By then their eyes had adjusted to the night. There was enough light from the stars and city for them to see. It was glorious. They lifted their faces to the lake's breeze, then he took her hand and they walked.

Along the way, they met a few other people who were walking the shoreline in the night. They spoke briefly as people do in such places and went on north. They walked slowly for almost an hour before they turned back toward his car.

He asked where she'd grown up.

"My parents and grandparents live in Texas. The rest of us are scattered around. I have a sister who's been in Chicago for a while. She came up last month and has stayed. Where's your family?"

"Mostly downstate. Some here in Chicago. My family all are somewhere in Illinois."

"That's very unusual—for you all to be nearby." As she walked in the swirl of the waves spending themselves on the sand, Tate watched her red-painted toenails, which looked black in the night. She thought of her sisters and cousins. "Most families are separated—out and around the country—by job opportunities and career moves."

"I've been shifted around, too, but I love Chicago. I've traveled extensively for business, and for pleasure, but there's no place in all the world like this town."

"Only a native would call this sprawling city a 'town' that way."

He agreed.

It was a beautiful night. The breeze was a light, lifting one, with the smell of the first elusive hint of fall to come. They could hear the calls high above them of the first migrating birds, already flying south. Although it was still only August, the summer was ending.

The wind played with the material of their clothing and teased their hair. Bill's glances were on Tate often. He saw that she was conscious of the night. She breathed deeply of it, her head up, turning, looking. She was one with the night.

He wanted her. His desire made him restless. His movements were a little quick and a little tense. He looked around, assessing who was in the area and where they were. And he monitored her. This woman whom he wanted. How was he to approach her? How does a man who wants to be a woman's prey make himself desirable to her? How does he encourage her to entice . . . him.

His car came into sight, and, in spite of his aching leg, he rather regretted it. But it had been a long day, and he had to take her home. He doubted very seriously that she would ask him up to her apartment, kiss him with matching hunger and take him to her bed to give him release from this mounting need of her.

There was always the chance she was the kind of woman who gave no warning and would just say "Okay?" or something simple and uncomplicated like that, but he doubted it. She seemed to him to be a woman who would need preliminaries.

That did annoy him. Her friend in Canada had taken Ned to bed in no time at all. The two women had seemed to him to be so easy. Knowing her now, he was amazed this was the same woman. What fluke had sent her up there to that resort? She'd made no bones about her interest in him then. Now she was treating him like an acquaintance whom she didn't actually dislike. Maybe that was progress.

He watched while she rinsed her feet in the spent waves, then he carried her to the car and tucked her inside, reluctant to let go of her. Then with an inner Jack Nicholson smile, he hunted out a tape of piano music with a skilled, good old dirty saxophone winding through it all. Sexy as all hell. He smiled. No sane man fights fair. The sound was like intimately trailing fingers on bare, heating flesh.

Neither of them spoke the entire way back down to her marina apartment. That music wove a madness in them so that their breathing was slow and they were each exquisitely conscious of the other.

With care he watched her with side peeks to see how he was doing. She relaxed, her head against the back-rest, her face turned so she could watch out the window as she idly toyed with the silk of her skirt. Unlike the blatant music, her fingers were discreetly sensual. He wanted them on him.

As they drove deeper into town, they left the windows open, because the lake breeze had invaded the city, pushing the heat of it southeast. Her hair was tumbled in the wind, and he wanted to stop and smooth it back, holding it from her face as he kissed her to wildness.

How was he ever going to survive if she didn't have enough common sense to take him home with her? Any woman who walked barefoot along a shore with a susceptible man ought to know he was ready, and she ought to be. But then again, he wondered, why had this woman been at that resort up in Canada? It just didn't fit.

He glanced over at her as she lay back in her seat so calmly, so remotely. So much about her puzzled him. She just didn't add up.

He had to stop for gas. He paid in cash, because he was barefoot, and didn't want to put his shoes on his sandy feet, and anyway his leg hurt. He got out at her marina complex and surveyed the area. Then he put his shoes on, and thinking that hope never fades, he escorted her to the lobby. She stopped at the door, and he knew he'd lost. This time.

"The picnic and beach walk were such treats," she said. "Thank you."

He recognized the Texas version of Mrs. Harris's polite-conversation segment of dancing school and the efforts of a diligent mother. He gave a brief token bow and replied nicely, "My pleasure."

Then she knew his thoughts and laughed. "It's so late. You have such a long way to go."

"Only down to the hotel condos on Michigan. Do you have a boat?"

"No. I took an apartment here only because I wanted the lake breeze."

"It must be a little cool in winter." He was embarrassed to be delaying so obviously. Why couldn't he just leave? "Good night. I've never had such a pleasant day." And he leaned over and gently kissed her mouth. No tricks. It was a straight, quick kiss, and he didn't lay a hand on her.

She responded briefly and smiled. "Good night." Then she turned away, carrying her shoes and purse. He stood there, watching her walk away from him, and from the way they spoke to Tate, he saw that security liked her.

So did he. And with luck he'd get her back to thinking as she had two months ago, when she'd first met him. He wasn't the same man he'd been then. He was aware of her now, and he wanted her.

He smiled into the night. It might take a while, but he had the time. With their business together, he had the excuse to be with her. He'd be very careful this time so that she would know he was willing.

And he'd let her catch him.

He laughed softly in his throat in a very male way as he stretched his body, moving his shoulders, pleased with himself. He felt his confidence rising. His body was strong and healthy. He felt very masculine. He was ready for her.

He did wonder why she was being hesitant. But that was all right. He could wait until she realized she was ready, too. She'd be worth a wait.

He finally got into his car and slowly drove to his own place. It felt empty. Even with the whole house staff roaming around, looking for things to do, he felt alone.

Three

___

It was after eleven that night when Tate passed apartment nine and tapped twice on the door. Her sister Hillary now demanded some indication each time Tate had arrived back at the marina. One little kidnapping, she thought, and Hillary, who was ten years younger, had been assailed by hovering traits. Tate smiled, then went to her own apartment.

Being terminally neat, Tate put down a newspaper, then, still not turning on the lights, she carefully undressed, dropping her silk skirt and blouse and her dainty slip and underthings onto the paper. She had learned at her mother's knee that like the last needles from the Christmas tree, sand seems to stay in a house forever.

Naked, she stretched, raising her hands high and standing on tiptoe, and she smiled through the dark apartment's windows, out over the lake, north along the shoreline, to where they'd walked. There was no way she could see that far; it was out of sight. Well, she was looking in the *direction* where they had walked.

Who would ever have believed that after having spurned her in Canada, Bill Sawyer would actually look at her and even kiss her? Not Tate Lambert. Never in this world. To think of the improbability of ever even *seeing* him again! Astronomical! It was spooky.

He was blatantly out to set up an affair. He was practiced in seduction. He knew the rules. He thought she did.

In this day and age, with all the risks, did she want to pursue this affair? He was thirty-eight. Hardly celibate. But she'd been with only one man. Her last intimate time had been almost three years ago, with her husband, Dominic, and he'd been so distracted, he'd simply used her.

How amazing it was that he'd been shocked when she'd divorced him. How could such a brilliant businessman have been so insensitive to a bankrupt marriage? She thought of all the times she'd tried to tell him and he'd appeared at first to listen, then he'd get up and make a phone call about something in his business, completely negating the importance of what she had said.

Was Bill Sawyer a lone wolf? He was equally committed to business. Dominic, too, had been attentive at first. He'd never been a womanizer—it was morally repugnant to him—but he'd been completely involved in the business world. A demanding mistress of another kind.

She and Dominic had slept in the same bed. But there'd been times when Tate would have sworn Dominic had been fleetingly surprised when he'd come home late from a meeting to find her in his bed. What sort of place did a woman have in the life of a man who could forget that he was married?

Dominic had a very tough family record, and because of his first wife, his trust in and value of women had already been tainted by the time he'd met Tate. His emotional life was guarded, and his heart locked away. Again, there were disturbing similarities between Dominic and Bill. She should pay attention. She didn't need another such experience; it could be a repeat of the whole terrible disaster.

When Tate had been pregnant with Benjamin, Dominic couldn't believe it. When he'd realized the child was a fact, he'd been almost afraid, as if he couldn't assimilate the fact that he would finally have a child. Not *they*, but only he. So after the divorce he'd taken two-year-old Benjamin—*his* child—and they both vanished.

It was then that Tate had learned that since the state court grants custody in a divorce decree, it is only the state court that can enforce the decree.

Tate hadn't seen or heard of Benjamin for two years as of last June 7. It was for her child that she grieved; her unnourished love for Dominic had long since shriveled away.

Her sister Hillary had devoted most of the past two years to searching for Benjamin, or searching for Dominic in order to find Benjamin. Only a man with limitless money or none at all could have vanished so completely.

As June 7 had approached this year, Tate had become desperate. She couldn't face the day. Her spirit had been ravaged, and she'd done a stupid thing: she'd talked her friend Julie into going with her to a resort for that weekend—a different place, with different circumstances, and completely out of character for Tate. There she'd first met Bill Sawyer.

She'd survived that weekend by stepping out of herself, and she'd survived her foolishness because the one man who could have interested her had been bemused by another, younger woman. How fortunate.

Or was it? Julie and Ned were to be married soon—once their respective respectable families could be eased into the shock of its suddenness. It *was* a little soon for them to marry, but they'd met that weekend and gone to bed that first night. How incredible!

So here was Tate—alone. Alone. Where was Benjamin? Where was her baby? She put her hands to clutch her hair and commanded herself to stop. Not again. *Never again* would she grieve so uselessly. She could cry a river and it wouldn't bring him back to her. She needed to distract herself and not wallow in the misery that was an open, black pit at her feet.

Tate grimly filled the tub and sank into the bubbles to deliberately turn her thoughts to Bill. She might just go ahead and have an affair. He would be willing now. She was attracted. He was—

Wait a minute, she thought. That was a very cold-blooded way of going into a relationship, to heartlessly use someone in order to be distracted. She ought not to do it. It wouldn't be fair.

She went to bed and cried herself to sleep. It had been a long time since she'd done that. This time it was a release.

* * *

When she wakened, very early in the morning, Tate lay silently. She considered her life and decided to change it. She had a lot of years ahead of her, and she was going to use them well. She got up and took the picture of Benjamin to the window to stare at it, then pressed it to her lips. Bury him? She groaned and put the picture away in a drawer under some sweaters. Out of sight.

Tate faced the fact that she had to give up the futile effort to find him. It wasn't fair for Hillary to spend her years searching. They could never counter Dominic's wealth. He would always be out of reach... taking Benjamin with him.

Tate faced the fact that she was thirty-five and not many available men were left in her age group. Okay. That eliminated marriage, and she'd already decided she wasn't a bed hopper, in spite of that one rash impulse. To go on and be one would taint her opinion of herself. So what was she to do with her life? She wanted to contribute enough to justify taking up her space in the world.

She was tired of the women's page. Well, while that wasn't true, what she really wanted was to get out of the series that had thrown her together with Bill Sawyer. She couldn't just have a brief affair. He could capture her heart. She understood that she could be hurt if she became involved with him. She'd dreamed of him last night. They were in the field behind her grandparents' house, it was spring, and they walked through bluebonnets. The sky was perfect, the scissortails swooping and the mockingbirds singing all the various bird songs. It would never do.

So that morning she called Robbie MacLean, wakening him. She told him, "I don't have time for the Sawyer interviews. I'm going to do the wives of the candidates, as you suggested. I want to move over into the political field, and this will be the perfect beginning."

"Attracted you, did he?" Robbie asked with some glee.

"Robbie, don't be ridiculous. It's too early in the morning to deal with such frivolous conversation. I am not at all attracted, and I really don't want to see him again."

"Whoa! Milady doth protest too—"

"Robbie," she said as a warning.

"He's from a delightful family. You must meet his dad. A nicer man you'd never want."

There was a tap on Tate's door. She said to Robbie. "Someone's here. I have to go. I'll do the wives, okay?"

"We'll see."

"Choose which ones. I'll get on it right away." Not giving Robbie any more time, she hung up and went to the door to peek, then opened it and let her sister inside. She and Angus were just down the hall from Tate. Hillary was carrying Angus's cat. "Good morning, darling—" Tate hugged her sister "—whatever are you doing up at this time?" Then she touched the cat and said, "Hello, Phoebe."

Hillary explained, "Angus had an early call. So I fixed his breakfast."

"Come have a cup of coffee?"

Hillary released the cat. "I've converted Angus to brewed, and he claims his whole outlook on life has changed."

The sisters exchanged a smile.

Hillary questioned, "Where were you last night? When you called to say you were going for supper, I thought you'd be home earlier."

It was true; Tate knew it fully then. She had bound Hillary to her with the search for Benjamin, and she must ease her sister away so that Hillary could live her own life. Loftily Tate admonished, "I'm your eldest sister, ten years older than you, and you ought to give up mothering me."

"I don't want to receive any more little notes in the mail saying you're missing. I aged twenty years in that time, so I'm now ten years older than you."

"I suppose you'll harp on that incident all the rest of your life. If I hadn't written that note, you'd never have met Angus. You should be grateful, and more lenient with me."

"I am," Hillary agreed. "He's a honey bear."

"Well, he's a Behr, anyway."

"Are you deliberately leading me astray from the subject?" Hillary lifted Phoebe from the table and leading me astray from the subject?" Hillary lifted Phoebe from the table and set her on the floor. "Uh, I hate to seem inquisitive, but where were you last night?"

"I was involved with a series for the paper, which I'm turning over to Ellen. I went to supper with the man who owns the companies the series is on, and we went up the lakefront to a private beach."

As Tate explained, Hillary brightened. "Really? He couldn't be in the doddering group if he took you to a beach—unless, of course, the chauffeur carried him from the car to the sand and the chauffeur's aide carried a rug to lay him on. Which? Did he walk by himself?''

Tate scoffed, ''Yes, of course.''

''Who is he?''

''I'll never see him again, so it doesn't matter.''
Considering the subject closed, Tate dispiritedly began to enhance her cereal. She added brewer's yeast, raisins, wheat germ, lecithin and bran.

As Hillary shuddered, the house phone rang and she picked it up. Even before she could speak, a marvelous male voice said in her ear, ''Good morning, Tate. It's Bill. Get all the sand out? I'm downstairs. Clear me with security?''

Hillary glanced at Tate as she gave a laughing imitation of Tate's ''Yes.''

Then Tate watched her sister say in a different tone, ''It's okay,'' before Hillary hung up.

''What's going on?''

''Bill's coming up.''

''*What?* How could you?'' She glared at her little sister. ''I've given him up!''

Hillary corrected her airily: ''Not . . . quite . . . yet.''
And she beat Tate to the door and flung it open without even checking to see what this Bill looked like.

Tate stood there, tousled and without makeup, very unwelcoming.

Hillary smiled as the newcomer came down the hall to the doorway, and she said, ''Well, hello! Come on in. You're in time for breakfast. I'm Hillary, Tate's youngest sister.''

Bill's glances went from a brief one to Hillary, to a shrewd one to Tate, then down Tate's body in its silk kimono, and up to her delightfully sleep-tousled hair. He'd had a quick call from Robbie, warning him that

Tate was in revolt. The cheerful reply to his call on the house phone had puzzled Bill, but now he knew to whom he'd spoken on the phone and why it had been the sister who had opened the door. He laughed out loud. He knew that if things went right, this would be the beginning of a long friendship with Hillary, but it might well be the start of a very tricky period with Tate.

Tate put her hands on her hips and said, "Look..."

Playing for time, Bill had reached down and picked up a willing Phoebe, who sniffed his chin. Bill looked around very casually, as if he were a welcome guest. "So that's the fish!"

That fact fascinated Hillary. "You know about the fish?"

Petting the preening cat, Bill replied quite easily, "I was there." His glance stopped at the unwelcoming expression on Tate's face. Without her heels, she was noticeably shorter. He felt dominant. He would have liked to sweep her up in his arms and carry her to bed. How fortunate that Robbie had called to warn him she was planning on ducking out; and that her sister had answered the phone or, he knew, he would never have gotten past security.

Hillary spoke again. "You were at the resort?" She glanced significantly at her sister. "Ahh. How interesting."

Tate put in sourly, "He was so completely taken with a very young redhead that he didn't remember my name."

Hillary shook her head at Bill. "How stupid of you."

Bill controlled a grin and shrugged. "Midlife crisis?"

Hillary loved it. Tate glared.

Phoebe mewed, and Bill turned his attention to the cat.

Tate saw that Phoebe liked him. But Phoebe liked men, so she was no measuring stick. Bill smoothed her fur, set her on the floor and ran a hand down her appreciative back. Then he followed Hillary into the kitchen, and Tate—the "hostess"—trailed after them. He looked around as he shrugged out of his suit coat and hung it on the back of a kitchen chair. "What's for breakfast?"

Hillary said, "I've eaten."

"You live here with Tate?" He hoped not.

"No, I live down the hallway, in nine, with Angus Behr."

"Mrs. Behr?"

"Not yet, but soon now. We're still getting acquainted."

He nodded, accepting that.

Tate sat down. Hillary indicated the cereal and said to Bill, "You can pass on that. It's so corrupted that it's healthy, and good for you." She opened the refrigerator. "There are bacon and eggs."

"Okay?" he asked Tate.

Tate wondered what she was supposed to say.

Since Tate took some time in her reply, Hillary gave permission. "Go ahead."

With no further hesitation and no apparent feeling of intruding, Bill undid his cuffs and turned up the sleeves a couple of notches. Then he washed his hands and took the bacon and eggs from the refrigerator.

As soon as he'd laid strips of bacon in the skillet and Tate couldn't possibly tell him to leave, Hillary airily scooped up Phoebe, said she'd see them later and went out of the apartment.

The fact that Tate ate slowly and stayed at the table was all that encouraged Bill. He set his plate on the table, across from Tate, then he sat down and buttered his toast. He sipped the delicious brew Tate had prepared earlier. "You must have been the one who made the coffee up in Canada."

"Kimberly did."

He raised an innocent gaze. "Kimberly?"

She gave him a patient look. "The redhead."

"Oh, yes." He remembered. "The kid."

She couldn't quite not smile. How could he tease her?

He chewed and swallowed, making relishing sounds. "I was starved. All's I've had in the last twenty-four hours was a light salad yesterday noon and ambrosia fed to me in a car last night by a lady of the lake."

"Your father kissed the Blarney stone," she guessed.

"'Twas me mither," he amended instantly, and took another bite.

"What are you doing here?"

He looked surprised. "Eating."

"Why did you come this morning?"

"Robbie sounded an alarm." He gave her a placid glance. "One always takes care of brushfires before the forest goes up in flames."

"Robbie told you that I want to do the political series?"

"No. He said you were copping out."

"I believe I shall sell him into slavery."

He straightened eagerly and inquired, "You believe in slavery? How terrific! I'll have to talk to your father as soon as possible. What do you think his asking price would be? Will he bargain? How does he feel about stocks and bonds—er, not those kinds—instead of ready cash? My liquid funds are a bit low right now. Have you ever been sold before? If so, why were you returned? Recalcitrance?" He said the last word slowly and looked at her with an interested expression as he took another bite, chewing and waiting for her to take the floor and speak, as he was sure she would, after that crack.

Coolly she inquired, "Is Robbie any kin to you? He, too, starts the day off-center."

"He really loves you. Do you realize that?"

"Yes."

"You're not going to be a coward and back out of the series, are you? You're not one to run away."

"I'm not running."

"Tate. What other reason would you have for quitting?"

"I want to start the political series. Ellen can do your people sitting on her hands. She's just out of school. An older woman." Remembering how he'd said the word "recalcitrance," she drew out each word of the last sentence: "At least two whole years older than Kimberly."

He had the audacity to laugh.

Snippily she urged him, "Hurry up and finish eating, so you can leave."

"Are you going to the office dressed that way? I love it, but I'd hate to see what you'd do to my staff. The women would tear their hair and spend the rest of the day in the rest room crying in despair, and the men would all be on their ears. Nothing would get done. I could cope, of course. Unless you'd smile at me." He put down his fork and scanned her blue eyes soberly. "Or if you would just look at me."

"You're coming on too fast. For a man who spurned me two months ago, you're being awfully pushy."

Very seriously he told her, "It scares me a whole lot that I was given this second chance and that I might botch it."

"That's nonsense."

"When a man gets to my age, he begins to sort things out."

"As you did in Canada?"

"Actually, it *was* a sorting out. I lost a very silly bid for a young woman who knew I was wrong for her."

"Do you really know that?"

"Yes. As I said, there comes a time when men see things clearly."

"Some do. Some don't."

He considered her words, wondering if it was he who didn't see clearly, then he asked carefully, "Who didn't?"

"My husband. He never quite remembered he was married to me. Not that he considered me a mistress, but he was surprised that I was around at all."

Bill stared, frowning, as he assimilated the fact that she meant what she'd said. It wasn't a complaint; it was true. "That's incredible."

"They say it takes all kinds to make up the world. I now believe it."

He asked, "Why were you in Canada." It was not a question but a leading statement so that she could know where to start and he could understand.

"That's too long a story for now."

Very slowly he said, "I'll wait until you want to tell me."

"Did you make the deal with Jennings?" She recalled that at the fishing resort the two men had been dickering over something.

"No. I don't need another business. He's a fascinating man. I went in order to judge him. I think he's a fine person. I'm glad I met him."

"Is he glad he met you?" With a fatherly protectiveness, Jennings had interfered between Bill and Kimberly, the redhead.

"I probably needed Jennings that weekend more than Kim did. It was a weekend out of time. Kim is a smart young woman. Her head is straight on her shoulders. That week, mine was a bit askew."

It had also been a weekend out of time for Tate. No question of that. If Bill, too, had been under stress, that made him more understandable. Had Bill's attraction for Kimberly been a grasping at straws? "I think I could dismiss you quite easily if you weren't so honest with me."

"I would never trick you."

She watched him, a smile forming on her lips. "How about the saxophone tapes, last night in the car?"

He grinned wolfishly. "That's not cheating. That's being smart."

"How did you know I'm susceptible to saxophones?"

"You dance. Your body feels music, so you had to like saxophones. The sound was made for you. And if you don't go get dressed right now, we're going to be very, very late getting to the office."

She groused, "I'm going to tar and feather Robbie."

"I'll coat him with wax first."

"How like a man to defend a man."

"I'll do dishes. Hustle up. Or—" he smiled "—could you use some help with your shower?"

"There you go again!"

He was shocked to his core. "I'm only trying to be helpful, and you, with your dirty mind, keep putting a different meaning to my words."

She gasped and couldn't think of a word of rebuttal. She turned away, lifting her hands above her head and shaking them to show her frustration. She walked out of the kitchen and into the bedroom—and closed the door.

He didn't move for a while but stood there, very serious and quiet. Then he rushed through the dishes, scraping them under the tap and putting them in her dishwasher.

Tate rinsed off in the shower, put on underwear and panty hose, then dressed in a blue silk shirtwaist and wound its tie around her slender waist. As she brushed her hair, she watched her face in the mirror and realized that Bill had made her feel pretty and desirable. How long had it been since she'd felt that way? She added makeup rather sparingly, slid her toes into pale blue slingback pumps, picked up a dull orange purse and went out into the other room.

He was combing his hair at the living-room mirror, and he turned to watch her walk toward him. He drew in his breath, his lips parting, for again it seemed that she meant to come *to* him. But she merely took her purse from the end of the table and put its contents into the new purse. She gave him a side glance, a little puzzled, then realized he'd thought she was going to him.

The flood of sensation that washed through her body was shocking. Deliciously so. She turned away as she realized she affected him strongly. She'd thought the things he'd been saying were a line. He couldn't have faked such a reaction to her; it had been too subtle. He wanted her—very badly.

She would have to be careful of Bill, for his sake. She turned and really looked at him before she smiled. He'd come there this morning so quickly that he hadn't shaved. He'd only dressed and hurried over in order to ward off her quitting. That was really rather endearing. With more kindness in her voice than she intended, she said, "I don't believe you shaved. Would you like to use my bath? I have a razor I use on my legs. I could even put in a new blade."

"I have a lavatory at the office."

"Of course."

"Ready?" he asked.

She glanced up at him. He meant ready to leave for his office. "Ready" was perhaps the most appropriate word he could have used for how she felt toward him. Reluctantly she replied, "Yes."

"Me, too. Let's go."

So again she got to sit and watch him drive his car through rush-hour traffic. He was one with the car, and the traffic didn't bore him. He was stimulated by it, alert, watchful, skilled. She asked him, "Have you ever been tempted to drive in a car race?"

"Not really. I was arrested going double the speed limit on a one-way, deserted, curving city street late one night when I was seventeen, and the judge urged that I attend defensive-driving class. My dad made me go.

"I expected to be lectured and shown gruesome films of mangled people, but it wasn't like that at all. They showed us how to survive. How to steer looking for the opening, rather than looking at the things to avoid. It was all good information. Everyone should take the course."

"That one time cured you of wanting to drive fast, to test yourself?"

"Tate Lambert, are you telling me you're a speed maniac?"

"No. But I thought all men had this macho image of fast cars and—"

"—whiskey and wild, wild women?" he finished for her.

"That saying goes back a long way."

He speculated, "When that was first used, it was 'cigarettes and whiskey and wild, wild women.' I think the wild, wild women came even before the whiskey was invented, and long before the explorers came to America and found the tobacco."

Tate said critically, "It implies that women are as bad for men as booze and tobacco."

"I'll drink to that."

"Hah!" Tate was indignant.

"Well, you did ask, and I have promised to be honest."

"What about the other way around?" Tate asked. "The women with tobacco, whiskey and wild, wild *men*?"

"I can't stand a boozing woman."

"It's all right if she runs about with a lot of wild men?"

He looked over at her. "If you really want to try it, I suppose I could wild myself up for a while. But it would only be to satisfy your curiosity."

She laughed. He turned his head quickly to catch her glance and share the laugh with her for that brief second. The blare of a horn and the squeal of brakes jerked him back to reality. He drove on a for a minute before he asked, "See? I've said all along that you're a wild, wild woman. Are you trying to wreck me?" He was serious.

She wondered if he thought she would take revenge for his having ignored her in Canada. "No. I'm trying to save you from yourself."

Understanding her warning, he replied, "Let me fly on my own. I can handle it."

"I'm not at all sure I can."

"Trust me."

"Trust a man who could fall for a tri-dye-haired, redheaded woman? You must think I'm mad!"

He gave a long-suffering sigh. "I suppose you're going to bring up Kimberly all the rest of our lives."

"She's a great jumping-off place for a good quarrel."

"You malign her. She never gave me the simplest nod, and positively no encouragement at all."

"That's why she makes such a good beginning to a quarrel. She wasn't interested, but you were."

"Just offhand, without puzzling it out, how many men have you known who dyed their hair three colors?"

"Not one."

"See?" he said. "She was my first sighting."

"Do you mean you wouldn't be jealous if a woman became entranced by a man with tri-dyed hair?"

He appeared to examine his soul while he assimilated the fact she'd just confessed she'd been jealous. With inner jubilation he said, "I don't *think* so. It would take an unusual man to dye his hair that way. I probably wouldn't feel at all threatened."

"Are you implying that I felt threatened by Kimberly?"

"You have to remember that she'd been at the resort for a week. With the cook drunk in the shed, she'd taken over the cooking and knew how to please a male palate. She was busy, pleasant, *she spoke kindly to us all*, and she asked nothing of us."

"You don't think I speak kindly."

He expressed great amazement: "How *ever* did you filter that out?"

"It seemed to me that you emphasized it just a tad."

"I suppose it was the Buick over in the next lane that was trying to bluff me at that very minute that altered my word sound."

"Baloney."

"You have a very interesting vocabulary."

"I was an English major."

"Honey, you must have majored in a lot of things."

"When I was nine, I tried to kiss my elbow so I could be a man and be Tarzan."

"Well, thank God you couldn't. I can't think of any pluses there could be in knowing Tarzan."

She considered, did he think there might be some pluses in knowing Tate Lambert? He could be very wrong. But for her to become involved with him would be a disaster. As the days had passed, the knowledge had loomed heavier. She was warned. He was not the hero type. He might have been at one time, but his ex-wife had apparently ruined any tendencies in that direction. A hero needed to be nurtured. He was disillusioned. If she was smart, she'd head for the hills and escape while there was still time.

Four

____

Since Bill had left his office with Tate just after lunch the day before, and now returned to his office with her and needing a shave, they were viewed by his staff with widened eyes. Tate was unaware; Bill grinned.

He'd never been a man who mixed business with pleasure. No woman had ever intruded casually into his working day, and that had included his wife. He ordered his own flowers, and he did his own shopping. He'd kept his personal life completely separate. But it was with some inner strut that he escorted Tate into his office and closed the door.

When he turned to Tate, Bill's eyes seemed to sparkle, and the yellow in his hazel irises appeared to leap like tiny flames. Tate blinked and looked at him a little more carefully.

His lashes came down about halfway in the most attractively smug male look, and he growled, "Do you need whiskering before I shave them off? It'll take my beard a good eight hours before it's ready again to whisker you."

She took a half step back, put one hand to her chest and gasped a credible "Sir!" But she was a little distracted by the flutterings that shimmied around in odd places inside her body.

Distracted that way, she really wasn't prepared when Bill took a step and turned his head just right to lean down and give her a quick kiss. "Good morning, Tate."

He'd been so quick about it that she hadn't had the time, and therefore the need, to do anything about the kiss. She looked at him a little owl-eyed.

"Come watch me shave." He undid his tie, unbuttoned his shirt and cuffs, and, with the shirt-tails still tucked in, he let the shirt drop around his hips, leaving his upper body bare. He did it briskly, as if it was a normal procedure.

That allowed Tate to accept his being half undressed, to take quick glances to see his strong arms and his wide shoulders and his hairy chest and flat stomach. His manner made it uneventful for her to lean in the doorway of the lavatory to watch. That's what she told herself, anyway. Why was it so fascinating for women to watch men shave? Her daddy used to be so amused by all his little flowers standing around him in the bathroom, their faces turned up to him as they watched him in fascination. And he'd dab their noses with shaving cream.

Bill rinsed his face and tested it for whiskers by feeling it with his fingers. He turned and looked at her watching him, her lips parted. Totally involved. He smiled at her in the most intimate way.

And to Tate it was intimate. There, with him half undressed and with her attention riveted to him in that way. He only looked at her, but it was as if he'd shared something very sexual with her. In just a look? How incredible. She couldn't take her eyes away.

Bill's whisker-seeking hand slowed, and it wasn't his face he felt. His gaze dropped to the lavatory as he tried to orient himself. He bit into his lip and looked at himself in the mirror, to smile ruefully, sharing his plight with his reflection. Then he made his hand pick up the shaving cream and spray a little into his other hand. He glanced over at Tate, then took a finger and dipped it into the cream and—in slow motion—put a dab on her nose.

She made a sound that was almost a giggle as she put her hand up to wipe it off, and she was charming in the doing of it. The efficient, self-sufficient Tate, acting so female. He laughed in a throaty, masculine rumble, and they shared the moment again in that strange way.

To prolong the intimacy, he was tempted to again cover his face with the shaving cream and begin all over, he so hated to break the spell, but there was no way he could eject the razor without putting in another blade, and his face couldn't tolerate a second shave right now. He'd done an exquisite job of the shave—there wasn't one whisker on his face that dared to peek over skin level—and the surface was getting a little tender. He was amused by his ploy, but for his face's sake he had to stop. He rinsed it off carefully, then opened the cabinet and considered his choice of after-shaves. He glanced at Tate, then took two bottles from the cabinet and let her choose.

She did that with careful thought and handed him one.

He used it sparingly and squinted at the sting of his overshaved skin, then he thrust his arms into his shirt sleeves, buttoned the shirt and held out his wrists for her to button the cuffs.

And she started to button them.

That pleased him, and he held very still, for he'd expected her to reject performing such a personal deed. He'd put his arms out in that way only in order to taunt her, for she was so independent, but she'd taken the request seriously and bent her head to do the buttons carefully. Her doing that for him touched him, oddly.

"Can you tie a tie?" he asked, his voice a little gruff.

"I can do a formal bow. With a regular tie, I don't always get the ends right."

He flipped his tie through its pattern of maneuvers without really paying attention. Jealously he wondered: Who was the man on whose tie she had practiced? Not her husband; he'd forgotten she was around. He didn't sound like the kind of man who would ask a woman to do anything for him in that way.

She had four sisters. No brothers. So who had it been?

A lover.

That was the only explanation. Jealousy shivered through him to clamp its talons on his gut. Damn the man.

Bill gave her evaluating side glances as he and Tate settled themselves at his desk. She could very well be exactly like his ex-wife and have had many lovers. He studied Tate intently and grudgingly admitted that she didn't look it. But she'd gone to Canada. There was that fact.

Being carefully casual but unable to keep the steel out of his voice, he commented, "It was very clever of you to take the tapes and boom box up to the resort so we could dance. Do you always do that?" He waited for her to betray herself.

"It wasn't so clever—"

Yeah. He thought so. It was an old trick to get into a man's arms.

"With five girls in the family we were used to entertaining. Boys did come around. I have some beautiful sisters—you've met Hillary—so there were always boys hanging around the house. Mother thinks time should be productive—idle time is the devil's, you know—so she had us teach the boys to dance. We taught most of Texas how to dance, one way or the other."

Snatching at that, he asked with cool indifference, "You teach men to dance...one way or the other?" His tone was heavy with innuendo.

She heard the tone and frowned a little as she hastened to explain, "No, not just boys. We've taught most of *Texas*, because—" She repeated it all, enunciating rather relentlessly, as if to someone who was unable to comprehend. "With five girls in the family, we've taught so many of the males how to dance that we've inadvertently taught the females of Texas, too." And she took the explanation one step more: "Because the guys would then teach the girls." She thought that Bill had turned oddly hostile, for no good reason, and he might just be a little dense, so she explained even further. "Like my parents teaching swimming down on the river. A kid drowned when they were growing up. It must have really shocked them, because they became very conscious of water safety, so they still teach kids to swim, down home.''

Bill reacted with no more than a single nod. He was coping with the fact that he might have misjudged her.

She was saying, ''If I'm to continue on this series, I wonder if we couldn't do a taped—''

He glowered, then interrupted. ''Of *course* you're going to continue. I won't do it with anyone else.''

She stared. What in the world? He'd gone from that tenderly sweet communication, of a kind, when he'd been shaving, to this?

''What *about* taping?'' He glared at her.

''It isn't important.'' She busied herself, needlessly shuffling papers, and wondered how to convince Robbie that this whole series had been a great, big, thundering mistake. The things she had to put up with in the male segment of society were appalling. She lifted her sullen stare to Bill to give him a raking, disdainful putdown.

He was staring at her as if he'd never seen her before. He was undoubtedly mad. Bill was just the same as Dominic. People who didn't live balanced lives became unbalanced. She was alone in his office, and no secretary—like that wimp out there in the front office—was going to come bursting in there when Tate's screams reverberated around the room. She stood up, placing the folders on his desk, discarding them, the series, him. ''Bill, I believe this is futile. I regret not doing the series—I think it would be fine—but I think you would do better dealing with Ellen, and I—''

''Now what in hell are you up to? I've never in my life met such a skittish woman. What's set you off?''

"What's set *me* off?" She watched him rise from his chair, but she didn't seize the chance to escape; she stood her ground and, gesturing, proclaimed, "Well, quite frankly I don't believe you're working with a full deck; you aren't stable, and I can't seem to get a handle on you."

He, too, was gesturing as he came around the desk. Right along with her last words he, too, was saying, "...can't get a handle on you." But he took her upper arms in his hands and held her there in front of him.

Again they stared at each other.

He snarled, "We'll probably marry and spend our entire lives this way. *Whose tie did you tie?*"

That question confirmed everything she'd been thinking, but she snarled back, "My own!" And since he appeared unable to cope with simple replies, she elaborated. "Some years back, women wore men's shirts and ties with their suits. I did, too. Ergo, I learned to tie a tie. Well—" she was honest "—not exactly. I never could get the ends straight, but I wore vests, too, and they covered the uneven tie ends."

In a normal voice he said, "Vests come in handy."

She nodded. His comment went along with everything else she was thinking, and she wondered if she'd ever get out of that room. But he wasn't actually violent; just odd. If she spoke slowly, explanations did sink in. "Bill, I want to leave now."

"No."

"Let go of me."

"Oh. Sorry."

He could be reached, she realized.

He asked, "How many lovers have you had?"

She was getting used to strange questions. First ties, and now lovers. She replied simply, "None."

"None?" he asked slowly, incredulously.

How complicated was "none" that he should have to question it? She chose not to complicate his understanding with a more elaborate reply. "None."

He moved away, went around the desk and sat down in his chair as if stunned by that reply. With him sitting and with the width of the desk between them, she decided to eliminate standing in the dominant position, and she, too, sat down.

"Then why did you go to Canada?" he asked.

She wasn't about to burden him with the ramifications of her life. If he had trouble grasping "none," there was no way he could cope with the complications of her life. So she said, "To fish."

He knew that she had fished. She'd explained the tapes and boom box—it was natural for her to share music with a group—and it had been a fishing lodge. Had she really gone there . . . to *fish*?

Since her answer seemed to surprise him, her curiosity won, and she inquired, "Why did you think I went to Jeb's place?"

"To look for a man. The way Julie had."

"I saw— Did you know Julie and Ned are going to be married?"

"Yes. Ned's an old acquaintance."

"Did you go there together?"

He seemed somewhat distracted, as if his attention wasn't on her words. "No, I went to meet with Jennings." He focused on her then. "We may offer him a place with us. He's an amazing man. Sharp, erudite, a gentleman. He wanted to sell me a company, or for me to buy in, but I don't need another. However, it was an opportunity to know him better and to see how he operates. I found him a sterling man. I was impressed."

She could not resist. "He was especially kind to Kimberly."

Bill grinned, watching her, then he laughed and shook his head. "So you tie your own ties, and you've had no lovers."

Flatly she put in, "I don't want to buy into your companies."

With a nod he acknowledged that, as he had with Jennings, he was interviewing her for a position. But he was so amused as he grinned at her that she smiled a little, and when he laughed, she did, too.

It rather amazed her that they settled down and worked in harmony. She discussed videotaping the interviews, which then not only could be used in his company as salutes to the various women—or integrated into a training program—but might well be added to the files in the public library. The interviews would cover training, education, setting goals, and it would be from the women. Bill was pleased. "Do you have anything pressing during the rest of this week?" he asked.

"No." She watched him as she slowly shook her head.

"Then let's get started. We can go to the plant in Alabama now, and I can set up two interviews for this afternoon. I think the plane's available. Just a minute."

"The plane...?" She was still questioning, but he was already on the phone to the pilot, then he punched out the Alabama offices, and within twenty minutes he'd set up the interviews and had the plane standing by, plus a video/audio crew.

Everybody scrambled.

Bill listened as Tate instructed his secretary to call Robbie and Hillary and cancel a dinner party with Petey.

"Who is this . . . Petey?" he asked.

She gave him a patient look. "A friend. Petrilla. What woman wants to be called Rilly?"

He nodded in understanding.

Bill drove Tate home. She'd already planned what to take, so he waited. He stood in her bedroom doorway. She ignored him, and he got to just watch her move. She was so efficient. So neat. She was ready in no time.

They went to Bill's apartment to leave his car and collect some clothes for him. He had clothes at his office, but he thought it seemed a good way to introduce her to the idea of going to his place. He wanted her to see it.

His condo faced the lake, overlooking Michigan Avenue. Bill's building had been a carefully constructed, ornate hotel that had been converted into condominiums. His condo had been his grandfather's suite of rooms long ago. The result was high-ceilinged, spacious rooms with charming plaster cornices. There were discreet colored-glass inserts in panels at the tops of the windows, and Art Nouveau lighting and railing ornamentation.

With the elegant flowing lines of the Art Nouveau accents, the rest of the furnishings could be of almost any style. Bill's taste ran to the rather subtle, with soft leather and suede combined with subdued-patterned handwoven rugs and plain drapes. The high walls lent themselves well to the display of magnificent, realistic, epic paintings.

Tate didn't have enough time to look around, since Bill had to pack and she helped him. He knew full well what he needed, he'd traveled so much, but it gave him pleasure to have her touch his things, and they had enough time.

They took a cab to Meigs field and the plane to Alabama. The company plane. Familiar with the costs of private planes, Tate knew the convenience cost a couple of thousand dollars for this flight—in fuel, pilots and plane care—but it was easier. In Alabama they were greeted nicely. No one cringed at the sight of Bill Sawyer. No one was obsequious. There was the right amount of ease and respect.

Tate found that interesting even as she was astounded that she had not yet fled. The last she remembered was her determination to quit and get out of his office. What was she doing with him clear down there in Alabama?

Well, for one thing, she was having a marvelous time.

They taped the two interviews. The women were interested, they handled themselves well, and they weren't fazed by the camera. Tate was astonished there were no rehearsals and no makeup people. The women just went on camera and started talking. Amazing.

Bill and Tate went to dinner with an assortment of pilots and film crew, along with a sprinkling of Alabama men who had clout. Tate noticed that Bill's crew from Chicago seemed up on what was going on in the organization, and they were interested in what was said.

The visitors had rooms at the hotel-motel that was run by Bill's organization for the local company's convenience. Tate excused herself from the table at about ten-thirty, and Bill walked her to the elevator to say good-night, but he returned to the table.

The next day the plane took Bill and Tate to Texas— Tate's home state. And after another interview and taping in Dallas, Bill gave the crews leave to explore, and he took Tate to visit her family.

Bill hadn't any solid idea of what he expected her people to be, but the ease of their lives did make an impression. He was aware only, really, of Tate. But he realized the house was big, old and solid. It was white clapboard, and the shutters were the traditional green. There were large oaks and some hackberry trees. He later remembered the two-story aviary with canaries and finches, but during that trip he mostly only saw Tate.

He did realize that Tate's parents were welcoming, in the easy way of people who are used to having guests. He was simply included. Their courtesy was automatic. They were delighted to see Tate. It was a loving family.

There was no question in anyone's mind but that Bill would stay in the big Lambert house. Her parents assumed this and Bill was willing.

Almost immediately Tate and he went across the open fields, where they were greeted by several horses, and then went on to see her grandparents. Bill was so intrigued at seeing Tate with her people that he paid scant attention to the family's position or possessions. But he did note that the Lamberts accepted him courteously but with no special attention.

They were used to men who courted their daughters.

"He isn't courting me," Tate said to her mother.

"Of course not," her mother replied.

"He isn't courting me," she told her father.

"No, not him," her father replied, and tousled her hair.

"He isn't courting me," she said at her grandparents' home.

"Who?" her grandmother asked, turning up her hearing aid.

"I heard you finally caught a fish," her grandfather commented. "I had another kind in mind entirely."

"I wrote to you about the fish myself and sent the pictures."

"He's a nice boy." Her granddaddy grinned.

"He is not courting me."

She didn't convince any of them. She'd forgotten how much she missed Texas.

Bill said Texas hadn't realized it was almost September and the rest of the world was cooling off.

Tate warned him, "If you say anything about Texas being the first step to hell so people can get used to being there, I'll—"

But he kissed her. It was the first time they'd been alone in years; to Tate it seemed like years anyway. He kissed her slowly, and his hands shook. Her insides shook, too. And after he kissed her, she couldn't remember what she'd been saying.

But she listened, wide-eyed and open-mouthed, as Bill asked her father, "What's your opinion of slavery?" as if he were consulting about the weather.

Her daddy asked, "Whose?"

Bill gave a serious nod and replied, "That would tend to influence the response."

And everyone inquired after Hillary. Where was she, and why hadn't she come home?

The best Tate could find to say was, "She's busy."

Since Hillary had been searching for children—and for Benjamin specifically—for the past two years, the questioners just assumed she was working. They had no clue that Hillary was now living "in sin" down the hall from Tate in Chicago. Tate knew it was better that the family didn't know.

Bill saw the pool that Tate's grandfather had blasted out of the riverbed years and years ago, when he was young. That was where the whole surrounding area's people had learned to swim.

Bill met Tate's sister Fredericka. She was a cheerful strawberry blonde who was between jobs, and to her Bill was a nonman, since he belonged to Tate. Tate ground out for the umpteenth time, "He's not courting me," but Fredericka only smiled.

Tate took him to a roadhouse that night with Fredericka and a silent bulk of a man named Sling who Bill thought might be the reason Fredericka was home between jobs.

The roadhouse had rough, bare plank floors with round wooden tables and wooden chairs. On the walls were laminated calendars from the past thirty-five years, and Tate told Bill the bar had been salvaged from a house of ill repute. The place had live country-and-western music, and a strong smell of beer was imbued into the very wood.

In slacks and a knit shirt, Bill was overdressed. He was also bareheaded. All the other men had on straw cowboy hats.

Tate gave Bill a smug smile. "Surprised you, didn't I."

He grinned at her. "It's just *great*! I've never heard such song titles."

The four drank beer, and the whole clientele taught Bill to line dance. It was a friendly night, and he met all the people who lived around there. Everybody knew everybody else. And they were curious about the man with Tate.

In the rest room, Tate said fifty thousand times, "He's not courting me," and got a good laugh every single time.

The one comment that caught Bill's ear was from a man who whispered to Tate like a steam calliope, "He's beats Dominic all to hell."

"He's not . . ."

But she whispered the rest, which made the "calliope" laugh uproariously and slap her on the back.

So that niggled in Bill's mind. What had she said he wasn't, in comparison with her ex-husband? His mind chewed on all sorts of ramifications of his imagination, until he was a little distracted.

Fredericka's Sling turned out to be a real surprise. He ran sheep and grew rice; and he was up on markets and on oil. He and Bill had a great deal in common—besides their being involved with two of the five Lambert daughters.

Bill really expected to see Sling take Fredericka out of that roadhouse for a while somewhere along in the night, but he didn't. At the end of the evening, the four drove in Sling's pickup with Tate tormentingly sitting on Bill's lap. When they arrived at the Lambert house, Sling said "Good night" in a final sort of way and kept Fredericka in the pickup while Tate and a frustrated Bill got out and went up on the porch.

There was an open porch that went all the way around the big house, and there were several swings. Bill was inspired. "Let's sit outside for a while and air out."

Tate questioned that. "Why are we airing out?" But she led him around the corner, out of sight of the pickup, and sat on the padded swing. It squeaked softly.

Bill explained, "I feel my pores are clogged with the smell of beer, a lot of sweat, and perhaps the spit-spread juice of some chewing tobacco."

"I think what you need is a rinse off, down in the pool. Are you game?"

"I . . . don't have a suit." Bill smiled in the dark. A classic opening for her to say, It's dark, and who will ever know?

She said, "It's dark, and Dad's suit will fit you well enough. Okay? I'll call Fredericka and Sling."

She ran to the end of the porch and called, "Hey, you guys . . ."

Bill thought: She didn't care *what* she interrupted.

So the two Lambert daughters fetched swimsuits and the happy foursome trooped down the way, across a field, and came to the swimming hole. Two other couples were in the water. The new arrivals changed in the bushes; Sling had had trunks in his pickup. They waded into the cold water, and it was glorious fun. They splashed and laughed and played keep-away. Then they lay on the bank, wrapped in towels, and talked for a while.

While they could still move and not just go to sleep right there, the four trudged back to the house. Bill expected to bathe inside, but the rest rinsed off the dirt under an open shower head rigged for that purpose, and he did, too. They dried off and hung the towels on the wire line. Fredericka kissed Sling good-night, and the other three went into the house, upstairs to separate beds, to sleep, flat-out and dreamlessly.

So it wasn't until Bill and Tate were on board the plane the next day and flying over Oklahoma on the way to Missouri, that he could ask her, "There was a man who said I was better than Dominic, and you said I wasn't . . . something. What am I not?"

She looked at him, astonished. Now, how was she going to say she'd said he wasn't courting her? She replied, "I don't remember."

Bill persisted. "He slapped you on the back. Whatever you said I wasn't made him laugh, and he had to've rattled your teeth with the slap. I almost throttled him."

"That was Pig."

"What did you say to him?"

"I don't remember. Pig had a pig when he was a little boy, knee-high, and he loved that pig so much that they finally called him that. He doesn't mind at all. He plays oboe with the symphony."

"Pig?"

"And Sling is in charge of the local Fine Arts Foundation. He brought the ballet to Kerrville, because no other man would get involved, but Sling's such a hunk that he had no problem with his name being coupled with the ballet. With Sling in charge of it, none of the other men minded going to the performances. Pig said it wasn't nearly as painful as he feared, watching people dance on their toes." Verbally, Tate had carefully led Bill away from the cause of Pig's hilarity. She thought.

They were landing in Chicago that night, after having collected another videotape and interview in Missouri, and Bill asked, "When Pig said I was better than Dominic and you said I wasn't...something, was that good or bad?"

Tate thought, it was probably the changes in altitude, what with flying around the country, taking off and landing that way and all, but she replied impatiently, "Oh, for Pete's sake! I told Pig that you weren't courting me!" She glared at Bill.

He looked astonished, then smiled a little and said a meek "Oh."

They landed, deplaned, said goodbye to the crew and caught a cab. On the way to Tate's apartment he said, "Pig didn't believe you."

She froze. She pinched her mouth. She clutched her hands, and she held her breath.

"Did he?" Bill pushed it.

She turned on Bill and snarled, "No, he did not. There! Now are you satisfied?"

He burst into laughter. He tried to stop—she was so furious—but he just couldn't.

Tate watched as Bill laughed with such good humor that damned if she didn't smile, then laugh, too. "Well, Bill, now listen. Do you know every single, solitary individual I met at home said *something* about your being there to meet my family? I did try to explain about the series for the paper, that we just happened to be in the area—and *nobody* would believe me. It was just maddening."

"If you'd told me, I could have saved you a lot of trouble. I could have set them straight."

Slowly, slowly, she wilted against the back seat of the cab and looked at her fingers. Yes. He would have told them how silly they were.

He said, "I'd have told them we'd just met and we aren't even sleeping together yet."

Startled, she looked at his face and gasped. "If you'd said *that*, the preacher would have come by within the first half hour. He'd still be lecturing!"

"What would be so bad about my courting you?"

She didn't know. She twitched a bit, then said, "We don't suit."

And he said, "Oh."

That's all. Just "oh" and nothing else. She thought, how spineless of him. It was just as well. She knew now exactly where she stood. He wasn't interested.

But then he kissed her.

She had been sitting there, wilted and separate from him, then she was pulled across his chest and he was kissing her witless.

It had been so long since she'd been seriously kissed. So long since she'd been held against a strong, hard, male body and felt the thrilling impact of female response to a male. It was a rare and wonderful thrill, and it swamped Tate.

Her emotions got a little out of hand, and she dug her fingers into his shoulders and made little sounds and took ragged breaths. Her body twitched, and she became a little teary.

Tate's eyes were still going in spirals when she and Bill drove up to the marina. The cabbie took out her bag. Bill told him to wait, and he carried it up to her apartment, took her into his arms and finished the job. He turned her brain into mush. Then he set her aside and said he'd be by for breakfast in the morning and he'd see her then.

After he'd gone, she took a long, deep bath, trying to reestablish the convolutions in her brain, but she went to bed, because the job was hopeless.

Bill Sawyer was really something. Perhaps, with care, he could be turned back into the hero type.

And in her lonely bed, she dreamed of doing that, but as a hero he wore all that hard armor and his horse kept pushing her aside.

Five

So on Thursday morning Bill came to Tate's for breakfast. Other than the fact that he looked like a prowling tomcat, he was very normal. But Tate was having qualms. She became rather formal and was carefully sedate as he kissed her.

At his office, and to her surprise, the two spent a fruitful day going over the interviews, planning final cuts. The women interviewed had been chosen not as *the* six superior women but for the variety of their skills. Bill had requested that aspect be emphasized in the series, because, he said, all the women in his companies were outstanding.

During that day Tate felt in control, for she had managed a reasonably professional relationship with Bill.

At dinner that night, in a small Mexican restaurant, Tate said thoughtfully, "I believe I begin to see why you were attracted to Kimberly."

"So tell *me*."

"She's like all these women. Young, on the threshold, bright, eager, excited by challenge, confident."

He looked astounded. "You mean I was subconsciously...recruiting? Do you mean my libido is *dead*? All I see in women is their potential as...management personnel?" Her instant, closed-mouth laughter was delicious to his ears. He watched as she continued to laugh at him, the lights in her blue eyes dancing.

She finally gasped, "Dead libido?"

He nodded solemnly. "And the only reason I'm investigating you is as a new member of my PR staff? I can only say that you are badly mistaken if you believe I'm trying to hire you for the organization. I have other intentions altogether. Swallow."

She did, slowly, and blotted her lips, then nervously licked them, her gaze never leaving his face. He moved his chair over, reached out and dragged hers closer, then caught her chin in his big hand and held her still while he kissed her.

Tate had never been kissed in that way. All her cells shivered in the heat, and it was a shimmy of delight, of excitement. To her ears, her nose sounded odd as it fought for air. All the rest of her was concentrated on Bill's kiss. On his mouth, his closeness, the male scent of him.

In little waves, sensations spread over her skin's surface. The pulsings sent strange and sensuous touchings to intimate places, causing intense awareness of herself as a woman and of her body's needs. It was thrilling. Her lifted mouth was like a small bird's coaxing to be fed with kisses, and her little, almost silent, sounds were the signals of female hunger.

All else around them vanished. He lifted his head to stare into her eyes, then his kiss changed to gentle sips that made her shiver deep inside her body. When he pulled his mouth away again, he touched her cheek with his fingers and smoothed it as he again stared soberly into her eyes.

They slowly became conscious of the applause, the whistles of appreciation and the soft laughter.

Tate could have died.

Bill grinned down at her with a hot, hot, stabbing look, then lifted his head and laughed at their audience. "It's our anniversary," he explained.

There were congratulations from the staff and guests in that small place. It was friendly, and there was a warm glow of camaraderie after that, with shared amusement and comments that caused more laughter. And then the chef brought out his boom box and they heard a Hispanic station's music. The atmosphere became quite festive.

Finally Tate could ask Bill, "Anniversary?"

"Each day is a day gained." His candor was real. "And that was an anniversary of our first kiss. I've waited all day for it. I waited all night just to see you again. I can't believe you're real. What was it that blinded me to you in Canada? There must have been some purpose in the delay to my being able to see you.

"I rarely have dinner at DeBoise's, where I saw you with your friends." His face was earnest, puzzled. "Why that night? To have seen you there was amazing to me. And I've been so afraid you'd turn your back on me; that you might not know how important this is, our meeting again. And to kiss you as I've wanted to since that night! You lifted the hair right off my head with this one. It makes me wonder what would happen to me if I could kiss you three times in a row."

She was silent as her body clamored for more, for the testing of three in a row. And she knew full well what would happen to him—and to her.

When he drove her home, she didn't let him go up with her. But she did kiss him. Twice. Her body reveled in being crushed to his, with his hard, tense arms banding her body closer to his. Her mouth was hungry for his. She held his shoulders, his head, and her throat made odd sounds.

And his hunger for her was stunning. She just about wrecked him as she tried to squirm even closer. She pushed away from him enough to gasp for breath and turned her head away from his. "One more," he coaxed for the third one.

"I can't."

"I crave it."

"It's just not a good idea," Tate explained breathlessly. "It's too soon."

"No, it isn't."

"Yes, it is."

"Tomorrow's Friday. Come sailing with me."

She hated to deny him, but she had to. "I must go to the office. My mail will be horrendous."

"Saturday?"

"Yes."

"Dinner tomorrow?"

She nodded. "I'll cook it. Angus and Hillary are coming over then. Come, too."

"I'd be delighted."

"About seven?"

"I'll be there at six-thirty, and I'll bring the wine. Okay?" As she agreed to that, he kissed her again, and all the erotic sensations rolled through them, and they barely survived.

Although she peeled him from her, she hated doing it. He was no help. She whispered, "It's too soon."

He didn't agree at all.

"Behave," she said, panting.

"How soon can I go back and discuss buying you from your father?"

"You're talking about a man who values his five daughters." She'd released one of his arms from her and begun to work on the other as the first arm went back to enclose her.

"Uh-oh, I can see the price going up. He did say he'd think about it."

"That only means he'll ask mother, and she'll be opposed." She'd gotten free of that arm and had begun to work getting loose from the other as his arm went back to holding her.

"There the price goes, up again," he said.

She laughed at him. It was a throaty laugh that made tickling sensations run down the length of him.

She asked as she struggled, "How many arms do you have?"

"I've lost count."

She pried his hands from her and opened the car door.

"Let me come up with you," he coaxed.

She shook her head. "Not this time."

"One more kiss."

"You're trying to confuse my brain."

"Do my kisses do that to you, too?"

Again she laughed, in that soft, intimate way, and he groaned.

"If you insist on going in by yourself, let me get you out of the car. It'll take a minute." He had to walk around the car three times before he could concentrate on opening the car door. He sighed very forlornly, but he smiled and looked at her with hot eyes as he took her hand.

She returned his smile, but she said, "Keep your distance."

"Yes, ma'am."

"Don't kiss me again, not even a little one."

"No, ma'am."

"I believe I like this new attitude."

His chuckle was naughty.

"What are you thinking, to laugh in that wicked, wicked way?" she asked.

"I—"

"No. Don't tell me. Just say 'Good night, Tate.'"

"Good night, Tate, my love. I'll see you tomorrow at six-thirty."

She stretched up and kissed his chin but was gone before his many arms could react and trap her.

At her office the next day, Tate tried to minimize her animation. She blushed because she laughed so easily. She noted that from a distance, Robbie watched her with hooded eyes and a slight smile. Why was he smiling?

A little before six-thirty that evening, Bill solemnly waited as security checked out the basket of wine and flowers he was carrying, then checked his identification. He was glad they were so diligent. But they seemed so curious that he inquired, "Do you have much trouble?"

"Not lately. We have an insurance investigator living here whose friends keep us on our toes."

Well, good, Bill thought. He chose the stairs, reached the second floor and saw apartment nine. Wasn't nine where Hillary lived with a man named Behr? He remembered her saying they were becoming "acquainted." He narrowed his eyes and wondered how he could convince Tate to allow him to move in so that they, too, could become acquainted. He might approach her, using that angle.

It was exactly six-thirty when he tapped on her door. And she opened it instantly, her eyes sparkling, her cheeks flushed. She made his soul reel. He was very pleased that his hand had sense enough not to drop the basket but carefully put it down on the floor before he reached for her. She didn't hesitate but came against him, and his spirits soared. His arms closed around her in the most amazing sensation he'd ever experienced. This was as it should be. She felt so good against him. So soft. She was perfect, and she smelled like a woman.

She smiled up at him with her hands at his nape and her body stretched up along his, allowing his hands the freedom to touch her. He ran his palms up over her hips, along her waist and to the sides of her breasts. She saw that the flames consumed the green bits of his irises, and it was as if she gazed into a volcano.

He was riveted. He wondered if he had ever been this taken with any other woman. Not that he could remember. He could think of nothing but Tate. He felt incomplete when she wasn't with him. He was in thrall.

Then he kissed her. His kiss was so hungry that he had to cup one hand behind her head to brace her poor neck against his onslaught. When she was a shambles—and he was trembling and his hands were shaking—he lifted his mouth to breathe roughly as he surveyed the wreck he'd made of her. She lay in his arms, her eyes almost closed, her lips pink and puffed, her cheeks now pale, her breathing erratic. He said, "Let's put a sign on the door saying that you've moved."

Her soft lips smiled a little.

He kissed her again. "Let's go to my place. We can leave your door open and put a note on the table for them not to wait for us."

She reluctantly stirred. "We have guests coming. We can't be rude."

"Are you involved with another man?"

"Of course not. I can only be interested in one man at a time."

Almost unable to breathe, he was so affected by her, he asked, "Who is the man who interests you now?"

Moving her lips with great difficulty, she managed: "You." But her voice was a whisper.

It was the most erotic sound he'd ever heard. He kissed her again, and again. He was in the middle of the terminal third kiss when the door was pushed open and a cheery Hillary and a man appeared. They stood and smiled at the interrupted couple. It was seven o'clock.

While Tate wandered around, a little vapidly loose-limbed and completely disoriented, Bill's computer brain filed Angus Behr's name, his black-haired, green-eyed countenance and the fact that he was a maritime insurance investigator. And Bill recalled security's having said there was someone in the building whose friends kept the marina guards on their toes.

Bill stood with his hands in his trousers pockets and his gaze on Tate while Hillary saw to the meal and flowers and Angus organized the glasses for the wine. "Good year." Angus approved of the wine.

Bill also thought this was a good year. Angus and Hillary exchanged a glance and laughed indulgently.

Both sisters were in end-of-summer dark cottons, and the men took off their jackets to hang them in Tate's coat closet.

Bill managed to come out of his stupor.

Then Tate almost surfaced. "I have some snacks, but don't eat too many. I have a soup that's been imbuing all this day, lots of soup, and you'll make pigs of yourselves."

"A soup?" Bill smiled a little. "Soup on this hot day?"

Tate explained, "It's a cold fruit soup. You'll love it."

They were sampling the shrimp and cold oysters, and Angus appreciated the wine. For the ladies Bill probably could have bought Strawberry Kellercup. But both men took the time to savor the wine. They rolled it on their tongues and concentrated on the taste. Bill thought Angus's appreciation of the wine almost made up for the tiny sip that Tate used simply to moisten the pastry puff she was chewing. Well. He didn't need a wine taster.

After the fruit-and-cucumber soup, there were chicken crepes and a spinach salad with hot, perfect rolls. A neighbor on the fifth floor had made them when Tate had kept her bird for a week, and Tate had frozen the perfect rolls for an event. For tonight.

"Does she make bread, too?" Hillary asked with interest.

"Not that I know," Tate replied.

Angus said, "She's the one."

Hillary explained, "She used to make bread for Angus, and it was perfect. Why do you suppose she hasn't made any for you lately?" She slanted a saucy glance at Angus.

"I have no idea." He grinned at the smug Hillary and slowly shook his head at her, chiding her for her sassiness.

Angus and Hillary helped clean up before they wandered off, leaving Bill and Tate alone.

Bill watched Tate, and she smiled. Moving carefully, as naturally as he could, he took off his tie and unbuttoned his collar button. She came over and helped. He sucked his breath in and went rigid. She watched his eyes as she gently but relentlessly began to tug his shirt from his trousers.

"Tate..."

"I stopped at a drugstore this noon."

He realized that she'd prepared for him all day. "Oh, Tate..." Her name came on a rush of shaky breath.

"If I'm hurrying you too fast, I can control myself. Maybe. I think I can."

"Never mind."

"All they had was blue. Will that revolt yo—"

He gasped. And then he was still. But in spite of a real effort for control, he began to laugh. He tried not to, but he couldn't help it. He sputtered, "Blue?" And then he bent back, laughing.

"Bill, now look..."

He hugged her to him, but he was still laughing.

"I don't believe you're taking this in the right manner. You're supposed to be serious and intense. This hilarity is messing up the whole deal."

"I know, but blue? Surely there was another place?"

"All the pink ones were gone. There were some polka-dot ones, but I hesitated."

That set him off again.

And she finally smiled. "There is an interesting variety from which to choose, but I couldn't be so rash." She shook her head. "Fascinating." She began to chuckle. He was wiping his eyes. She asked, "You really don't mind?"

"It just so happens that I have some plain, utilitarian protection for us. I was of the same mind. But I have to see the blue one."

"I couldn't buy just one."

"How many did you get?"

"There was a special."

His grin began to widen. "How many?"

"I didn't have much time, you see, so I had to take what was there, and these were on special. I think an introductory offer."

"How many?" he insisted.

"Fifty."

"I like the way you think."

"You needn't feel you have to use them all up at once."

"—and all blue?"

"Yes. I opened one and looked. They're a little loud. Bright."

He was having trouble again. He kept his mouth closed, but his shoulders shook and his breathing was labored. He gave up and laughed. "I can hardly wait. You're a precious woman."

"Then I haven't embarrassed you?"

That sobered him instantly. "No. How could you think that? I'm very touched you'd want me. Tate, a woman who prepares and plans to love a man is giving him a lovely gift. Thank you."

"And you can handle blue?"

"I'll have to see. I keep getting this...mental... picture, and I...find it...hilarious."

"It could well look a little eccentric."

That set him off yet again.

With their laughter easing their movements, Bill and Tate had actually made it into the bedroom. He saw that it was neat and orderly. The bed was wide and smooth. Tate was awkward. He realized she wasn't used to intimate relations with men.

As he very naturally continued in the removal of his shirt, he told the motionless Tate, "You're probably the most graceful woman I've ever seen move, and I've watched a lot of women. Women are the most miraculous of God's creatures."

That charmed Tate. Maybe he wasn't the bulldozer she'd thought him.

Then he blew it. He teased her: "It's never been any wonder to me that men have collected women in harems. Each woman is so different. Think how it was for a man to be the sole functional male in a room full of women. To watch them and to choose one. I can hardly wait to negotiate with your father." He grinned at her.

"Hah!" But the exchange had dispelled her awkwardness. They were back on an equal footing of give-and-take. She felt that and wondered if he'd said all those things with calculation so that he could achieve just exactly that. Was he that clever? This problem solver, this mover and shaper, this negotiator, this power man?

So, along with his complexity, and his potent maleness, he intrigued her.

He removed his belt and unzipped his trousers. She was mesmerized. She watched as he took off his shoes and socks, then his trousers and briefs. He moved around as he did so, completely at ease. He was simply taking off his clothing. He was naked. He turned to her. And she got an attack of nervous doubts.

He put his hands on his hips and watched her stare at him. And he inquired, "What do you think? Will the blue make it?"

She slowly grinned, her stare broken, her glance rising to his eyes. "You could do anything," she told him. "You could even wear the polka-dot ones and look magnificent. You'd make it seem the only way."

He was smart enough to resist giving a flippant reply just then, and his chuckle was so intimate. He came to her unthreateningly. He took her face between his hands and leaned down to kiss her in sips. Gently, sweetly, tenderly. His voice was husky as he told her, "You're breathtaking." Then he hugged her to him and was silent.

Tate could feel his thundering heart. She could feel that he trembled, and it was very certain that he wanted her. She knew he was being careful with her, and she was touched by his consideration. It had been a long time since she'd been with Dominic.

She put her arms around Bill's waist and hugged him back. Then she nudged him to be allowed to pull back, and although he was reluctant, he allowed it.

She looked down at his eager body and said, "We have a problem. I would like to be closer, but there's a barrier."

"I know."

She raised her gaze to his and asked, "What are we to do?"

"It seems to me I've heard something about this. Yes, I do recall hearing there's an ancient custom that solves just this very thing."

"Really?"

"Yes. It appears unbelievable to the uninitiated. Weird, even. But I've heard it works. Are you willing to see if it will at least . . . help?"

"Well. I *would* like to be closer, so I suppose I'm willing."

"Let's get this pretty gown off."

"That does it? Just taking off my dress?"

"It's just the beginning."

"Well, I didn't think the blue material was thick enough to . . ."

He flung back the spread, the cotton blanket and the top sheet, then he patted her bare bottom and encouraged her to move onto the bed. She crawled over past the middle, and for a while he had to look at the ceiling.

As he started to crawl after her, she said, "It hasn't helped yet."

Still on hands and sprawled-out knees, he leaned over her and kissed her. "You're supposed to tell me I'm awesome."

She looked into his hazel eyes, which seemed filled with yellow fires, and she whispered, "You are magnificent."

"Awesome," he corrected her.

"Exciting."

"You're beautiful, just beautiful. You make my brain spin as it tries to keep me going while it copes with my reaction to you. It's being strained to the limit just keeping me from falling flat with reaction. I think it's drunk with love."

He kissed her some more, lying beside her, his hands moving on her naked body, brushing, kneading, touching, fingering and making her shiver as she raised her knees and restlessly rubbed them together in little whisperings.

He told her she was lovely, and he touched her as he told her where and how lovely. His hands were hot, and his breathing was rough.

She moved her own hands, and once she stopped to whisper, "This isn't helping. The barrier is getting worse."

"That's part of the weirdness. It's supposed to happen that way."

"Amazing."

He corrected her again. "Awesome."

"Fantastic."

Their kisses steamed, and their hands scorched. She thought he had to be part dragon, because his breath burned. His body became filmed with sweat and shivered, and his hands trembled. She began to moan, and his throat rumbled in response. They writhed on the hot bed, the aching mounted, and finally he put on the blue shield, and it looked amazingly sexy.

He eased down, she was so ready for him, and he sank into her heat with a groan. Sweating, panting, he paused, holding back, waiting until she started to react, then he began to move. Exquisitely. Slowly.

Changing position. Deliciously, marvelously, he thrust into her.

He kept the pace slow and easy as his sweat ran and their bodies slithered. But she began to gasp, to clutch, and he thrust hard, and again and again. And they went right up that magical spiral to its peak, to float for that impossible, ecstatic, thrilling pause—before the free-fall.

For ten seconds he lay, spent, then he levered himself onto his elbows so that she could breathe. It was a long time before there was any other movement.

She agreed then to the label he'd demanded: "Awesome."

He replied, "Mmm."

After another long time, she said, "You took a great chance using a blue one. What if I'd laughed?"

He assured her, "It still would have been great—just different."

"You are awesome. You take such care of me. For me. You're very sensitive."

"I love you, Tate."

"I find that hard to believe. But I'm glad you care about me."

"You'll come to realize and understand my love. I have all the rest of my life to convince you."

He kissed her in tiny, cherishing salutes. He smiled into her eyes, and she allowed her fingers their freedom to caress his hair, to slide along the rough silk of it, before she ran her hands over the shape of his head.

He parted from her reluctantly, and she made sounds of protest. He lay beside her, cooling, his eyes sleepy as he smiled at her. "I'd never realized there really could be a perfect woman."

"Thank God I could never kiss my elbow."

"Well, I guess so!" He was appalled. "Why would a woman like you want to be a man?"

"I don't want to be...now. It was when I was nine, and I wanted to be Tarzan."

"Ah, yes."

Then curious, she inquired, "What did you want to be when you were nine?"

"Nine is too long ago. I suppose I wanted to be GI Joe or something strong and destructive. I played a lot of baseball."

"Were you any good?"

"Most of the time."

She watched as her fingers rearranged his sweat-dampened hair. "What else did you do at that age?"

"There was a little blonde who was just the cutest thing. One night I climbed out my window to go see her. Nobody was around. The streets were deserted, and the houses were all dark. It was so quiet. Eerie. My dog was nervous. Imagine a cowardly dog! So we went back home. I had a heck of a time waking up my brother Sam to go down and open the door for me to get back inside." He sighed, but he grinned at Tate.

"You've always noticed girls."

"Yeah." He said that with satisfaction.

Tate gave him a smiling look that chided him. "I think you're addicted."

He laughed and pulled her close. And he said, "Thank God."

Six

Tate and Bill lay in her bed, smiling at each other. Contented. She could let her fingers touch his hair just as they'd longed to do. And she could look at him. It was unbelievable that he was there with her. That he wanted to be there and that they had shared such a marvelous encounter. Was it truly love? She studied him, taking pleasure just in being with him.

Bill was pleased that she was interested in him and wanted to touch him. It was a plus that she did. He was still afraid that her attraction to him was nebulous. He needed time to concentrate her attention to him. He wanted her.

She was exquisitely formed. She was so smooth. His hands were pleasured by the feel of her. Her long legs drew his glances, and he had to raise himself onto one elbow so that he could run his hand down her hip and look at her.

As he'd shifted to lounge by her, he watched her as she had moved so that she lay relaxed, her shoulders flat to the bed, her head on one pillow, her hip turned toward him and one knee bent rather modestly. Her body was lax and soft. The exquisite centerline of her was a lovely, eye-capturing curve. Her navel was a dimple, and the lush, richly dark curls at the apex of her legs were beautiful.

His look followed the line down her body, then came back to the watching eyes. He curled his hand and laid it along the side of her face for a cherishing minute. Then he gently brushed her soft lips with his thumb and ran it along her jawline. He put it on the pulsebeat at her throat, then slowly drew a line down the center of her body between her breasts, to the indentation of her navel and farther. He watched his thumb and saw her body. With his hand spread wide on her he asked, "What Master Sculptor made you?"

He looked into her eyes, and they smiled in their mutual pleasure. And he moved his hand on her, his intent gaze following it in slow appreciation. Her breasts were rounded, and the nipples were perched there like candy kisses, waiting to be tasted. He tasted them. After a savoring time he lifted his head.

Tate looked at him. His eyes were more yellow than green. His smile was different. Her lips parted in a silent gasp, and her fingers paused in their dreamy pettings along his nape.

His voice was husky as he told her, "You are a thing of beauty."

He shifted and stretched up to give his concentration to her mouth as his hand kneaded her pliant breast. Under his working palm, her nipple became soft and puffy and her body began to feel restless.

Tate loved the way his tongue tilted with hers, and his kisses were deep and tender. Coaxing. Wooing her. He was so male. He gave time to salute her eyes, her chin, her throat, rubbing his hard face and the beginnings of his beard growth along her tender flesh as he marked another difference between them.

His mouth went to her ear, where his tongue curled through the delicate shell before his firm lips tugged on the lobe and he breathed so that erotic shivers ran through her body.

Her hands moved on their own. Her knees rubbed together, and she couldn't breathe through her nose as she tried to get more air. Her body curled toward him and stretched to give him access to her. And she was astonished that she could want him again so soon.

He smiled, and she heard his murmur of encouragement in the sounds men have made in their throats since God gave Adam Eve. Alluring sounds so sensual that they curled her body to welcome his. Sounds of promise, sounds of pleasure that said no other woman was so enticing. Sounds that made her want to hear more, cause more. Tate knew it was the sound of enticement, telling a woman she is where she should be and he'll take care of everything. She should just allow him his way and everything would be all right.

Bill lay along her body, and his was hot and hard. He had her trapped under his moving hand and his strong, hairy leg. She stretched and pressed against him, and his chest rumbled with his pleasure. She spread her hands on his shoulders and pressed her fingers into his tense muscles, then rubbed her palms along his hard back and in the thick, rough silk of his hair.

He teased her with his hand and played his fingers over her. He tugged and smoothed. He suckled and tasted. He kissed and licked. And she began to twist and pull at him, panting.

He lifted his shaggy head. His breathing was deep and fast, his body very interested in hers. He scrubbed his hand along her curves and up over her tautened breasts, pushing and kneading, and he grinned at her. His eyes were all yellow fire as he asked in a low and wicked rumble, "What do you want?"

She opened heavy lids and looked at a complete barbarian. That was what surprised her. He was no longer the urban sophisticate. He'd reverted. She looked past his head and saw that they were indeed in her bedroom, but she looked back at Bill and saw a very basic man. But then, she felt very basically woman. She smiled with her puffed and reddened lips as she allowed her eyelids to almost close. She moved her shoulders just a little, in a very female way, to make him aware of her, pinned against the bed as she was by his body, and she said, "You."

He laughed with the laugh of a man whom a woman has pleased. Then he scooped his arms under her body and rolled over so that she was on top of him. He smiled up into her face and said, "I'm yours. Do your damnedest."

She didn't know what to do. She'd never before been given the freedom of a man's body. She could do... anything? She asked, "I may... touch you?"

And he realized she was an innocent. She'd been married all that time, and all she'd had was sex. She'd never made love to her husband. And Bill was thrilled. He was really her first lover. He smiled in delight. "Be my guest."

She couldn't immediately pounce on him, Tate knew. She ought to be subtle. She leaned over and kissed his mouth. He was amused, she saw. He lifted her so that she sat astraddle his hips, and he watched her as he put his hands on her breasts and worked them with his fingers.

With him holding her in that way, he was limiting her. She busily took his hands and put them up behind his head. She had a tough time doing that, because her breasts jiggled close to his face and he lifted his mouth and suckled each in turn. So she had to put his hands under his head and make him keep them there before she could pull away from his greedy mouth. He laughed.

As she began to move down his body so that she could tongue his nipples, she realized the barrier was also limiting her movements. It was then that she saw her position was exciting to him. So as she worked on tonguing his ear, she moved her hips and slid up a little and allowed her breast within the range of his mouth as if she didn't know it.

Then, of course, she had to turn and look at the rest of him, to move so that she could investigate a different aspect of him, but she was distracted by those hairy thighs and the tense muscles. She had to bend over and see if she could soothe them with long strokes of her soft hands, but that didn't help. And she contemplated the barrier. She could now touch it and examine it and its location and movements. She had to hold it and move it and exclaim. And she had him riveted, his sounds strangled, and his attention very concentrated.

She turned around and asked, "What on earth is the matter with you? Why can't you hold still?"

He laughed and lifted her and solved his problem. He turned her and lay on her and with stern discipline he controlled himself as he teased her with slow, easy strokes. Then he parted from her and played with her and encouraged her to know him. Intermittently he would take her with marvelous strokes and touchings, but it was a long, sensuous time before they ecstatically climbed the final, thrilling spiral and touched the edge of paradise.

It was after midnight when she wakened him. He didn't want to go home. She said he must. She had to sleep, and if he was there, she wouldn't. He grinned and said he could understand that, since she had finally agreed that he was awesome.

With his barrier controlled at last, they could get close and hug for a short time.

"I never said it was a permanent cure," he warned her.

"I'm so glad it isn't." She had her arms wrapped around him, and she smiled up at him.

He had a hard time leaving her. But he didn't coax her to let him stay, for he knew she would have allowed that, and when he did stay over, he wanted it to be her idea. He said, "Why don't I call my sister and arrange for us to drive down to see Jenny tomorrow? It's been a while. Would you go with me? I never know what to say to her."

Tate suggested, "You ask questions. And you tell her what you've been doing and what you think about things."

"Moralizing?" He made a face.

"No. Just about what you see, jokes you've heard. That sort of thing."

"How do you know that?"

"It's what my parents do with children. They taught us to do that. It's what I do with the children at the library tapings."

After a time he said in some surprise, "That's what my parents do with everybody."

"It might not work with Jenny the first couple of times. When you tell the jokes, don't do a one-man, stand-up improv. Just tell it, not expecting any reaction. You'll be surprised."

"What sort of jokes does one tell a twelve-year-old?"

"Funny ones." She grinned at him.

Bill called early, and Tate was still in bed. To lie there with her eyes closed and his voice low and rumbling in her ear was exceedingly erotic to her, and she laughed.

Her laugh was marvelously intimate, so close in his ear, that Bill groaned and said, "I wish I were there with you this minute. Are you in bed?"

"Yes," she murmured.

So he told her what he'd do if he were with her—where he'd touch and where he'd tickle her just the tiniest bit.

She said he was a scandal.

He said he'd never been this way before he knew her and he thought she was leading him down a primrose path. And what *was* it about primroses that was so wicked? Why did young men get led along such paths and become ruined when all it was, was roses?

She had no idea.

So he said to get that delicious body out of her bed before he got there, or they'd never get down to see his daughter. They were supposed to be there for lunch, and it was already after nine.

For their visit to Bill's daughter, they wore casual clothing. Tate was in white slacks, a sleeveless top and sandals. Because summers are peculiar in the North, she took along a large designer scarf to put around her shoulders.

They took U.S. 34 out of Chicago to Princeton, a charming small town about two hours south of Chicago. The pair were more than lovers. They had much in common, and they talked all the way there, about one thing or another. At one point Tate asked Bill, with some curiosity, "Do you suppose your interest in young women could be misplaced paternalism? The working out of your guilt for not being closer to your daughter?" She expected him to huff and scoff.

He was silent for a long time, and Tate thought that perhaps she'd offended him. Then he said, "You may have something there."

Tate found that Princeton was a pretty town and a nice place for a family to grow up. Bill's sister, Carol, lived in a new area. Carol's house was large, set on enough land so that it appeared comfortable. Around it there were English flower gardens. There was a basketball hoop by the garage, and a tree house, which immediately caught Tate's eye.

Carol was very pregnant. She came to the door to wave her greeting but waited there for them to get out of the car and come to her. Jenny was nowhere in sight. Hugging her brother, Carol explained, "The kids took their bikes down to get ice cream. Jenny made you a cake." Carol kissed her brother's cheek and looked expectantly, avidly at Tate. "Hello," she said with a welcoming smile and great, great curiosity as her husband, Bob, came along the hall. He was a big, easy man, sleepy eyed and calm.

Bill had explained to Tate that Bob and Carol had a daughter Jenny's age, and three younger sons. The two girls were good friends. For Jenny, living with her aunt had been ideal.

They settled in for a visit. A couple of Bill's brothers came over with kids, and Jenny and her cousin returned with the ice cream. Jenny was a marvelously gangly twelve-year-old with braces on her teeth, and she was so unconsciously beautiful that Tate was charmed. Tate noticed that Jenny was excruciatingly self-conscious with her father. Bill was easier with the little nephews.

The meal was two casseroles served with fruit and vegetable salads. There were rolls and jam, and there was Jenny's cake. It was delicious. Having been warned it was Jenny's cake, Bill had two slices. Then he cleverly complimented his sister on it and was "astonished" it was Jenny's. And she laughed, hiding her braces behind her hand, but she said, "Beth helped with the frosting."

Tate was used to people, having come from a big family herself. She helped with lunch and the cleanup automatically. But Bob and the brothers pitched in, too. They didn't just sit and let the women do the work. They organized the table and monitored the kids, and the chores went effortlessly.

After a lazy time of just talking, there was a basketball game with lots of teasing and rude remarks and laughter. Tate noted that Jenny was pretty good. But the baseball game was the thing. There was enough room in the backyard, so the family divided up and played. Tate watched and cheered. Carol was too pregnant for any excitement.

Tate asked Carol, "Why did you let us come down? You didn't need all this company."

Carol smiled. "I love Bill, and I wanted Jenny to see him and be around him. They're so awkward together. They need time. And I wanted to see you. Bill just doesn't bring any woman around the family, and I about went berserk with curiosity when he said he was bringing a lady down to meet us. Is this serious? I hope so."

"We'll have to see." Tate was evasive. "You're really a fine woman to have taken Jenny in."

"No problem. She's a nice kid. The two girls are like twins. It would be tough to split them up." Carol gave Tate a thoughtful look.

"I have four sisters. It was a wonderful thing for us to have been together, growing up. Instant, constant, loyal friends."

"That's how it is for Jenny and Beth. They've had a great year together. They'll be friends all their lives. We were concerned at first whether it would work out, but there was never any conflict between them. It worried us for a while, that one or the other was adjusting and giving in; they seemed *too* compatible. We were so relieved at their first spat that we laughed— and they did, too. It was very nice."

"You must be unusual parents," Tate remarked.

"Bob is an unusual man. Every night I thank God I found him."

And Tate said a soft "Wow" in heartfelt awe.

Carol agreed. "He's the one. A miracle. He likes kids, but he loves me and he'll put up with anything if it makes me happy. So I'm very careful not to take advantage of him. And I take very good care of him.''

Tate looked at Carol. "Is that the secret?"

Carol smiled. "I think you have the basic ingredients. Bill would walk on hot coals for you."

"Oh, no!"

Carol laughed. "That proves it all. He would, but you wouldn't want him to. So find him another way to prove his love."

"Do you really believe he loves me?"

Carol gave her an interested look. "Even if he didn't look at you to share anything said or just to check on you, as he is doing this minute, the fact that he brought you here is enough."

Tate looked out to where Bill was playing second base and smiled at him. He laughed and almost missed the ball. That brought hoots of derision from both sides, which amused him.

When the game was over, the men came over to drop onto the grass by Tate and Carol. Bill held Tate's ankle in one hand as he listened and talked to the others. He told Jenny, "I played ball as a kid. I lost a whole game once—not only that game but the whole tournament. I was the last batter."

Sam contributed: "I wouldn't speak to him for a week."

Bill groused, "You still remember that? You could have forgiven me by now."

Sam shrugged as he vowed, "I'll remember to the death."

Bill looked over at Jenny. "Do you realize you're kin to that man?"

And she laughed out loud, not even covering her braces-filled mouth. Her eyes danced, and she was delighted with the exchange.

Then Bill said to her, "You really figured Josh in the last inning. You positioned perfectly for the play. If his swing had been true, you'd have had him."

Tate saw Jenny glance up at her dad, and she looked so pleased. Although there had been no such play, Tate saw that Jenny had realized her dad understood that she knew what she was doing.

Bill said, "When you bat, try moving your hands up just a little for balance."

"I agree," Sam said.

"Who asked you?" Bill asked in disgust.

And Sam reminded him, "I wasn't the last batter on August eighteenth, twenty-three years ago."

Jenny asked shyly, "You were fifteen?"

Bill nodded.

Jenny looked at him for a minute before she blurted, "What did you do?"

"I struck out. I didn't even come close."

"What did you do then?"

"I bawled all the way home, and Sam rode my case, and Mother made me a chocolate cake."

Jenny became pensive. Bill knew it was the word "Mother" that had done it. Had anyone ever made Jenny a chocolate cake to comfort her?

Carol distracted them by asking, "Jenny, why don't you show your dad the tomatoes you've grown. He might like to take a couple back to Chicago."

On their way back north, Bill was exuberant. It had been the best visit he'd ever had with Jenny. He was so pleased, he couldn't get over it. He made Tate wonder what had happened the other times. It had seemed like an ordinary visit to her. Why did Bill think this had been so different? Different in what way? But she didn't press him for details. It wasn't any of her business.

But on their way back through Chicago's Miracle Mile of shops, Tate suggested they stop at one of the shops. Bill found a parking place, and they walked to one of the name boutiques.

Bill was tolerant and relaxed to endure...and to pay. He managed to conceal his shock when he realized Tate wasn't buying something for herself but something for him to give to his daughter and his niece.

Tate chose dresses that were specifically for each girl's coloring but were similar in style and for similar occasions. They were wrapped, and Bill enclosed separate notes to Jenny and Beth. Tate then chose a fall skirt and jacket for Carol, to give her a goal to shoot for after the baby was born. On her card Bill wrote: "To an elegant lady."

He took Tate back to her place, and as she opened the door of apartment six, he said to her, "I love you, Tate."

"Why ever for?"

"Because you're a fine woman. You're changing my life. You're solving the problem-solver's problems."

"How?"

"I think it's with magic."

When she scoffed at that, he took her to bed to prove it was magic, and she had to agree. She thought, how could it be magic when they were now familiar with each other? How could it seem new again when it was simply the coupling of two bodies? What an amazing gift was love.

His kisses were so sweet. Magic. And his body was marvelous. A miracle. He held her as if she was precious to him. As precious as he was to her. And her will melted to his, and she allowed him to do anything he wanted.

He held her, and she moved her body to excite him. He was excited. He kissed her, and she touched his lips, then his tongue, with hers and his breathing roughened. How did such a simple thing set him on his ear? It was indeed magic.

The bed moved as they did, and she wrapped herself around him. She squirmed, and he reacted. She touched him and he groaned. She moved and he gasped. It was marvelous.

Their bodies heated and strained, and they panted as they tried to get impossibly closer. Their passion mounted, and their brains were swamped by the sensations that flooded them in thrilling waves. As their ecstasy became exquisite, they left this universe entirely and flew beyond time to paradise.

When they lay, spent, she murmured, "I'm becoming partial to that shade of blue."

He gave her a lazy smile. "I swear to you I didn't even notice the color this time."

"There's a kind of yellow-green one that would go with your hazel eyes. I believe I'll get some. It would probably be stunning."

He was incredulous. "Yellow-green? You josh."

"I think it would be gorgeous."

"Are you using me for a color scheme?"

"Why else?" She raised questioning eyebrows.

Since he'd just shown her magic, it took some time to show her why else, and it was just as good with a

plain, utilitarian one. Before he slept, he muttered,
"See? Color has nothing to do with it."

"Yes, it does," she replied softly. "You make me
see all sorts of colors. I even feel them as they pop inside me and spread the most marvelous champagne in
my cells. You're awesome."

And he was touched to the core of his being. He
held her gently and cherished her.

It was Sunday when Bill and Tate finally went sailing. It was a memorable day. They borrowed Angus's
boat, fixed their meal and ate on deck. They decided
to ask Jenny and Beth up for the next weekend.

Out on the water in the partly cloudy day, they were
completely alone. Tate mused that no one who hadn't
lived in a city knew the glory of being alone. It was as
if there was no other human around. There was only
the wind in the sails and through the ropes. There were
no voices but their own. The only indication of other
people were the buildings crowded in a tiny line along
the shoreline, and there were other, distant sails.

Alone.

He gave her wine with lunch, and she drank it as she
would have iced tea. It made him smile, and she
thought how cheerful he was. He peeled off her
swimsuit and kissed her excited body, her sensitive ears
and her eager mouth. He teased and played with her
until she turned the tables and began her own teasing.

When he was panting, her eyes widened as she exclaimed, "I forgot to bring some protection."

But he had. She said she was disappointed it wasn't
blue.

They cleaned the little boat, tidied it nicely, and
sailed it back to its berth. Bill gave Angus a bottle of

1961 Château Lafite-Rothschild as a thank-you and suggested privately, "Since the sisters' palates are...untrained, you might get Hillary her own bottle of wine."

Angus just laughed and said Hillary was a beer drinker.

Bill replied, "That figures."

So then later, Bill asked Tate, "Do you like beer?"

"Not very well. I rather like that wine you've been giving me. I really don't mind it at all."

She "rather liked" the wine, he thought. She "didn't mind" it. He began to understand about time and women who tried men's souls. Ah, and she could try his soul all his life, this precious woman. He went to her and held her close to him with love. It was different from his hungry embraces, his yearning ones.

And Tate was conscious of the difference.

Bill didn't stay with Tate that night, either. He had become reluctant to be separated from her. And he was restless when she wasn't close by. He knew he loved her. But this wasn't just love. This was getting into something he'd never experienced. It was much, much more serious.

Seven

On Monday when Bill came by for breakfast, Tate was subdued. As he kissed her, he saw that she was a little wan and pale. So he leaned back to assess her mood as he grinned and inquired cheekily, "Rough weekend?"

She nodded without speaking, leaned her forehead against his chest and stood against him, her arms around him loosely as she absorbed his presence.

With a new sensitivity to females, brought home to him just that weekend and from seeing Jenny, Bill realized Tate's mood was different. Whatever it was it was serious. He ignored the fact that they were already running a little late, and he held her gently, coping silently with and denying his desire.

She understood. She knew how she affected him. And she would have led him into the bedroom, but he made no other indication of need. He held her gently, not moving his hands, just holding her.

"Tell me," he said.

He showed his concern with his hands as he smoothed back her hair and kissed her forehead. He hugged her closely.

He touched her heart. No one but parents knew when to do that. Sisters could give vocal support and maybe a pat or a quick hug, but only parents or someone who loves... Did Bill love her? Or was this something like his feelings of protectiveness for Jenny?

She leaned back and looked up at him. He was serious. His watchful eyes searched hers. "What's wrong?"

"Nothing, really. I just... I miss my little boy."

"What little boy?"

She parted from him and moved toward the kitchen. He followed, asking again, "What little boy? Yours?"

"Yes." She began to fix their breakfast.

"What happened?"

"After the divorce, I won custody, but Dominic took him and they've disappeared. I haven't seen Benjamin in two years. Two long years. Two years ago last June seventh."

Bill made a sound of sympathy in his throat as he thought: June 7? June 7? *That*'s when she'd been in Canada. Had she fled there? He looked at her, alert and listening, but she said nothing else.

He knew about her husband, Dominic. Dominic Lorenzo. A name that made men's eyes change. Having been given an in-depth dossier on Lorenzo, why hadn't he heard about the boy? He would rattle some teeth for that oversight. Of course, he hadn't asked about children. So Lorenzo had stolen Tate's child. "What's he like?"

She dropped a spoon with a clatter, hurried to the bedroom, pulled opened the drawer and scooped up the picture of Benjamin. She carried it back to the kitchen and stopped before Bill to open her hand and give Benjamin's picture to him.

He saw that the child was a healthy boy of about two who laughed at the camera. Tate's child. Bill had never been overly interested in children, but this was Tate's child.

"Did you hire someone?" he asked.

"Of course. I did all the usual things. Nothing worked. The state has jurisdiction on custody cases. The FBI is involved only in federal cases, and kidnapping laws don't apply in custody fights. Hillary has spent most of these past two years hunting stolen children. She's become almost an expert on travel, where to stay, who cooperates."

Tate looked at Bill then, in an accepting way. "I've given up. I will pretend he's somewhere safe and that I'll see him again someday. I can't allow Hillary to spend her young years in fruitless searching."

Tate had been very normal up until then, but now her face crumbled as she said in great agony, "I miss him so terribly. He's such a sweet little boy. Who takes care of him? How do they treat him? Does Dominic pay *any* attention to him? He rarely even realized I was around. Would he give any thought at all to a little boy who says only childish things?"

She put her face in her hands and turned her back to Bill. She had never meant to come apart, to burden him.

He went to her and put his arms around her. How to comfort her? he wondered. "Tell me about him. How old is he?"

She almost babbled as the words flowed. "He's such a nice little boy. His eyes are so full of fun. He will look at you and melt your heart. He is really very..."

She was so earnest, her eyes watching him as she gestured and tried to make him see her son, that she touched his heart as he listened to her tell of Benjamin.

He knew child snatching from one parent by another was all too common. He could make inquiries. He wouldn't mention to Tate that he was making any effort, because it probably wouldn't make a difference. Why get her hopes up?

They were late in getting to his office. Tate continued to be unusually quiet and a little withdrawn. She replied to his comments, and she would smile, but he knew she was suffering—this woman who had given up her child to time.

During the week, while working on the interviews, Tate managed to get to the greater task of organization. She sorted and pared down the staggering amount of information she had gathered. Then she began making a cohesive sequence of the interviews.

At first she and Robbie had planned to cover the series in six issues of the *People's Voice*, but the women's training and experience were so informative that he opted to present them in a pullout. The rough looked great, and he and Tate decided they would make it available at cost to colleges and technical schools as outside reading.

Tate had been especially pleased when Robbie had volunteered to send copies of the paper to the Chicago Public Library and Cultural Center. They would supplement the tapes of the women's interviews that Bill had donated to the center.

Quite by happenstance, Tate learned that the original videos, taped on that impulsive flight around the country, had been preliminary filmings. The women had viewed them, gone over the material and made it more succinct before a final film had been made.

Knowing that helped Tate. One evening when Hillary was there because Angus had to be out of town, Tate told her sister, "The fact that the women hadn't asked even to rehearse or outline what they were going to say was simply stunning, but even more boggling was the fact that not one of those women had even peeked into a mirror! If someone had come into *my* office with a camera that way, I'd have dived under the desk."

"That's natural," Hillary agreed. Then she said, "I'd like to see the contrast in tapes between the first, impulsive ones and the prepared ones. How they speak, how they sit or stand, whether they move or just talk naturally. That in itself would be instructive."

"And their makeup. Especially around their eyes. Un-made-up eyes look like fried eggs, because the brows block the sun and the skin is white above and below the eyes."

"Where did you see that?"

"On me," Tate admitted.

"Must have been a jolt."

"It was. But those women had no real warning, and not one of them turned a hair. It was a great relief to know that hadn't been the only filming. For them to have been able to do something like that, so casually, would have made such women too... formidably diminishing to me. It was a relief to know they were human, too.''

"Are you feeling human? The invincible Tate Lambert?"

"Hillary, I've given up on finding Benjamin. I don't want—"

"No! We'll find him."

"I can't have you using up your time on something so fruitless. In two years we haven't even come close. I love you, Hillary. I can't take any more of these years from you. You've found Angus, and you need to make your own life."

"Angus understands."

"For now."

"That's a tacky thing to say about him." Hillary's eyes flashed.

If nothing else had clued Tate to Hillary's love for Angus, her defense of him certainly did. She smiled at her baby sister, "Are his intentions honorable?"

"He wanted to get married as soon as you were found, but I don't think either of our families would have accepted the fact that we'd just met and gotten married that soon. We're thinking about getting married down at home during the Thanksgiving holiday. How deep are you in it with Bill?"

"Floundering."

"Do you love him?"

"I'm afraid so."

"Why are you...afraid?" Hillary narrowed her eyes and frowned.

"He's a power, just like Dominic. He, too, has had a failed marriage. Would he lose interest the way Dominic did? I couldn't go through that again."

"What was your basic impression of Bill's daughter? Was she hostile to you?"

"Not at all. Aloof. But she's twelve, and that would be natural. She and Bill have never had much time together. So they're awkward. Being with her aunt and uncle has been ideal, and her cousin Beth is like a sister to her. It was a tough life for her before Bill got custody. Her mother is a sleep-around. But there's more to it than that."

Hillary didn't say anything for a minute, then she shook her head and took a deep breath. "People have such troubles. We were lucky to have had our parents."

"And our sisters."

"I would like to find Benjamin for you."

"I know you would." Tate looked out over Lake Michigan. "I've set my mind to accept that he is safe and that someday I'll see him."

Hillary burst into tears. "I can't stand to see you so torn."

"Oh, love, I never should have involved you in this. You're too tenderhearted. I'll survive. I'm very strong. But, dear heart, I release you from this quest."

"Are you sure? Think about it for a while, and we'll talk about it again in a couple of weeks."

"No. Let's finish it. I can never repay you for these two years."

"You and your key found Angus for me."

"Lucky, lucky Angus."

On Friday, with their project almost done, Tate and Bill left his office and drove to her apartment. It had been a long week, and they were both tired. Tate had some steaks marinating in the refrigerator, a salad to toss, and the last of the perfect rolls.

Bill said, "I thought we'd go out to eat."

"Oh? Would you rather? I can keep the steaks marinating another twenty-four hours—we won't need knives."

"I thought I'd take you out and ply you with wine and bring you home and make love to you."

Tate replied with rather elaborate astonishment, "I hadn't realized you wanted me in your bed."

He made his eyes cross.

She went over and sat on his lap. "I can't cross my eyes. Do it again."

He did, and she was properly impressed. She asked if he could curl his tongue, and he possessed that additional talent. She was amazed. Then she saw that he could roll his tongue over. And she told him that ability was genetic. Did he know that? He accepted the information without undue shock.

She coaxed him to roll his tongue again, then she put her tongue to touch his. He didn't mind. She kissed him—touching that talented tongue with her own in a lovely caress—and smiled as she watched the yellow in his eyes flame up. She kissed him again. He shifted and adjusted her on his lap, then inquired, "Are you indicating that you're going to allow me a little afternoon delight?"

"It's evening."

He considered all she'd done lately. "You've worked very hard this week. Are you tired?"

"Very."

"Poor baby girl." He rubbed his hard fingers up her spine and then dug them nicely into the tensed muscles at the base of her nape. As she moved her body in its pleasure, he put his other hand at the top of her chest to brace her against his rhythmic kneadings.

Out of the corner of her eye, she looked over at him, licked her lips and mentioned, "I could use a long, slow massage."

"Oh?"

"I'll have to take off my top so that the material doesn't bunch and wrinkle," she told him.

"What a good idea."

"And it might be better if I lie flat. Would it be all right on the floor?"

"How about the bed?"

"Why, of course! Now, why didn't I think of that?"

So he led her to the bedroom, where he meticulously removed her hampering clothing. Then he began to discard his own.

She questioned that. "Do you expect me to massage you, too? Why are you taking off your clothes?"

Unhesitatingly he explained, "Massaging a woman is sweaty work, if it's done right. I'm just saving on cleaning bills."

"Oh." And she nodded with the sense of it.

He found a thin, faintly scented oil in the cabinet in the bath. It was not an oil that would cause the fragile condom to deteriorate. He returned to her bed with a lecherous smile to lay her flat as he knelt over her. He did an exquisitely slow job of smoothing the oil on her nude body. His hands took special pleasure in the feel of her. Some parts of her got more oil than others.

She reminded him, "My elbows."

He was curious. "Elbows?"

She languorously opened an eyelid to murmur, "Halfway between my wrist and my shoulder."

"Right. Here?"

"That's my breast."

Smoothing the firm round sensuously, he explained, "You said between your waist and your shoulder."

"My wrist. I said between my wrist and shoulder."

"You want something between your waist and your *soldier*? I was in the air force. Will that be okay? You want a little oil between us?" He moved his oily hand in slow, lingering circles over both her breasts. Her nipples were lush, puffed and glistening with the oil.

"A flyer?" she inquired.

"I was in the last of the lottery for Nam."

She frowned. "Did you have to go over there?"

"No. The ponderous wheels of the government grind slowly, and once set in motion they have a hard time stopping. For me it was just an inconvenience. They had stopped the war by then, but I did learn to fly. It is a pleasure. The old saying that it's an ill wind that blows no good is true." Then he lifted both oily hands and rubbed them on his hairy chest.

She lay watching him, and a little smile curled the edges of her mouth. "I could do that." And she reached.

"Not yet. I haven't done your back." He turned her over and began afresh, pouring oil into his palm, rubbing his palms together, then laying them on her.

She made soft murmuring sounds and lifted her foot to rub it against his back as he straddled her.

He said, "Cut that out. You're trying to distract me."

"I was trying to oil your back."

"I'll show you how to do that in just a minute."

The line of her spine fascinated him. He drew his thumb along its length, then he smoothed the line with his oily palm. He rubbed her shoulders and her bottom and the insides of her thighs. He had to move around and concentrate. Her sounds, the way her body moved and the feel of her had him riveted.

He stroked the length of her and swirled his hands on her firm bottom, his fingers parting the globes. He lay on top of her and moved his hairy body on her oily back, as his hands continued their work along her sides and along the puffed rounds of her squashed breasts. He slid along her bottom and between her thighs. His body was rigid and hot, and the oily texture was thrilling for them both.

He got up from her and turned her over. He looked into her eyes, then down her body. He smiled at her and winked. She lifted her arms, and he lowered himself slowly to her. And as he lay on her, her body opened to him and welcomed him intimately. Her arms and legs enclosed him, and they made love. It was a sensual sliding and especially titillating. His massage had heightened her awareness of him, and his loving was slow and hard. It was different and special.

The massage was so relaxing, they'd had to sleep for a while. The phone wakened them.

Tate picked it up and said, "Hello?"... and the receiver slid right out of her oily hand. She had to grope for it and try again: "Hello?"

Hillary replied, "One can only hope one doesn't interrupt anything. There's a bunch of us going to a farewell-to-summer free concert at the public beach. Why not come along? It'll be interesting."

"How soon?"

"Half an hour?"

"I'll let you know." She laid the phone back and turned her chin to her bare shoulder to look back at

Bill. His hair and tanned skin were dark against Tate's pale pink, lace pillows, and he was watching her with lazy hazel eyes. He smiled like a lion whose tummy had been rubbed just right.

She told him snootily, "I did most of the work."

He replied gravely, "It's part of the scheme. You tone *all* the muscles, not just a few, select ones." He was rubbing her hip in a nice, soothing way.

"I didn't realize the research was so in-depth."

"I was." He looked so amused, so smug.

She shifted to face him, lifting the sheet, and he helped by moving, his hands adjusting her. Instead of just facing him, she was against him, and he kissed her.

When they reluctantly parted their lips, she asked, "Would you like to go to an end-of-summer concert at the public beach?"

"No." He settled a little more firmly in bed in order to indicate just where he wanted to be.

"Somehow I expected you to say that. It was Hillary. She and Angus are going with some of their friends."

"That's nice. Who's playing?"

"What?" She was distracted.

"Which orchestra? Bands?"

"A whole slew. Ragtime, jazz, reggae, some sing-along." She wiggled a little comfortably, indicating she wasn't interested, either.

"Let's go," he said.

Now, that did amaze her. But she called Hillary and said they'd be there. They stripped the bed sheets and remade it, then they showered in a rush and dressed. By now Bill had moved a selection of his clothes into her apartment. They put the steak back into the marinade, grabbed a turkey sandwich and made it in just a couple of minutes over the allotted half hour.

The four took a cab south toward the public beach until they came to a cheerful crowd. They left the cab and walked along and—quite amazingly—found their friends.

Tate heard Hillary whisper to Angus, "Mark was over there."

"I saw him," Angus replied.

"Who's Mark?" Tate asked.

"He was one of Finnig's men who helped us to find you. Finnig apparently has people who watch over us now. He's a strange man."

Tate said musingly, "I believe there *are* no normal people. I've yet to meet any."

While both Hillary and Angus professed to be normal, Tate just laughed at Bill, who was standing with his hand on his chest as a prime example of normality.

The bands were in pockets of devotees. In the loose group made up of the Behr friends, the four danced around the fringes of the clustered people. They stayed together well enough, and they had a marvelous time.

At one point, when it was an easy thing to do in that crowd, Bill said to Angus, "How about meeting for lunch at my place?" And in an undertone he added, "We could discuss Dominic Lorenzo, and I might get a handle on Benjamin."

Angus looked at Bill. "We've done a little research ourselves. Nothing."

With those words Bill knew that Angus had already tried to find Benjamin. "Would you allow me to hire you as a consultant?"

"I'd donate my time. I just don't want you coming in too wide-eyed and innocent. Some heavy brains have come up empty."

"I would appreciate being briefed. Don't tell Hillary or Tate. I don't want to raise any false hopes."

"Tate's given up," Angus told him.

"I know."

"Okay," Angus said.

"Let's try for Tuesday. My place?"

"Thank you."

"My pleasure."

Saturday morning Bill drove down to fetch Jenny and Beth back to Chicago for the weekend, to the delight of Bill's mostly idle house staff. The cousins stayed at Bill's, but they went swimming at Tate's. Jenny swam nicely. She and Beth were very alike, and both girls were tall for their age, as Tate had been at twelve. And they slouched. Tate didn't mention it, but she was conscious of her own posture.

Jenny especially appreciated the size of the plaque for Tate's legal-sized fish. She grinned at Tate, then shook her hand. It was the first true understanding of the episode of the fish that Tate had shared with anyone. Tate was especially pleased with Jenny's handshake.

Bill took them to lunch at the Art Institute, and they walked through the Picasso exhibit. Jenny and Beth had brought their gift dresses along, and wore them to dinner that night at DeBoise's, where the two peeked around to watch people. The girls were charmingly careful about their manners. Bill noticed that and smiled at Tate to share, and Tate was captured.

Then, later, the two cousins watched as Bill gave Tate a chaste good-night kiss, and left her at her apartment.

On Sunday they went to the Museum of Science and Industry, which was almost entirely refurbished, and they were all engrossed by it. There wasn't time for the Field Museum. They had dinner at Tate's. Hillary and Angus came, too, and they brought Phoebe, the cat. Everyone was comfortable. All four adults were used to children, and they directed their conversation to include the girls, talking about things that would interest the children.

Bill drove the cousins home early Monday morning, so he reached his office late. He called Tate at the newspaper. "Jenny talked to me a little on the way there. It was easier with Beth along. She's a good kid. Jenny and I are starting to have things in common."

"She's a lovely child."

"I think she's coming along very well, considering."

"Considering . . . what?"

Bill hesitated just a little, closing down as if he hadn't realized just exactly what he'd said, he was so unguarded with Tate about himself, but this was about Jenny's circumstances, so his words were empty. "All she's gone through."

That night Tate had just arrived at her apartment when Bill arrived. He held her hungrily, crushing her to him. "Did you notice I hardly touched you at all? I have to let Jenny get used to you. She has had so much of that—sex, men sleeping over with her mother—that I don't want her to think we're like that."

"I see."

He loosened his arms so that he could see her face. She didn't lift her head, so he had to bend his sideways in his effort to see her expression. "What's that mean?"

She lifted a bland, nothing gaze and said, "I understand your not wanting your daughter to think you're bedding me."

"Hold it. Now, just a minute, Tate. Don't read back-street, sly, inadmissible sex into this. I'm just trying to show her there is such a thing as discretion. You do love me?"

"On occasion."

"Don't shut me out."

"Now, why would I do that?"

"You want me to tell her that I can't stay out of your bed? That it's agony for me to keep my hands off you in public? After all she's been through?"

"And what has she been through?"

"A mother who is an alley cat... who dragged my daughter around all these years because she wanted a good blackmail on my bank account. But I never knew she was so openly sexually active—with parties that must have been very puzzling to an unsupervised child, and were given by her *mother*."

He paced, running his hands through his hair. "My fault. I should have paid more attention. I was too concentrated on work to distract me from the kind of woman my ex-wife had become. She moved around the world, and Jenny must have been in five boarding schools before she was nine. When Jenny was at school, I'd call her and we would have stilted little conversations. I didn't go often enough to see her, and on holidays my ex carried her off to somebody's yacht or to ski. And Jenny was there to watch.

"Carol and Bob and I are very earnestly trying to let Jenny see there's another way to live. A normal way. A family way. I can't bring her to live with me. She'd be lonely and lost here in my place, even in a fully staffed house. Think how lonely she'd be." He flung out his hands. "How could I have been so blind? It must have been like that for years. And I wasn't sharp enough to realize what was happening."

"It happens right under the noses of a lot of startled people. We believe the best of people."

"I love you, Tate."

She only nodded. She was distracted, wondering what circumstances surrounded little Benjamin. What about him? Was anyone interested in his welfare? Was he eating right? Did he get sick? Who cared about Benjamin? Who else, besides her? Had he ever wondered what had happened to his mother? Did he think she'd just left him all alone and didn't care about him? Did he think about her at all? Where was Benjamin? Where on this earth was her little boy?

Eight

On Tuesday Angus arrived at Bill's place for lunch and found that he was a good host. Bill didn't rush him, but mixed them each a light drink. While Angus sipped his, he looked around and saw everything. He particularly liked the paintings. He indicated his approval with a nod after he had thoroughly studied each. He wasn't in any particular hurry.

After a time, having assessed the casual opulence, Angus asked with a stern look, "Aren't you a bit out of Tate's class?"

Bill gave Angus a slow look. "I hope not. Her family appeared to accept me okay when I met them in Texas."

Angus smiled. "You'll do."

It was then that Bill understood that Angus had a background similar to his own, and Angus would be comfortable under any circumstances.

There was a small solarium built on the southern side of the apartment so that the low winter sun could be captured to its fullest. And it was there—that summer noon—that Bill had had the luncheon table set. Since he hadn't known Angus or how much formality might discomfort him, Bill had chosen to lunch in the solarium because it was the least formal place in his apartment.

The drapes were parted, the balcony doors pulled back, and the panorama of the city lay below. Bill had tapes of soft, old jazz and blues recordings on low. There was a cool summer lunch set up on a cherrywood sideboard, and Bill and Angus served themselves.

When they were seated and comfortable, Angus began: "We've gone through the regular channels to find Lorenzo. Deeds, cars, employment. All the inquiries were routine, and they were useless. A man like Lorenzo who wants to disappear, can.

"He doesn't need to do anything himself, not even drive a car or own one. The ramifications of his businesses are worldwide. He can move from one of his houses to another, and no one knows about it. He isn't a criminal, in that he hasn't physically harmed anyone. He pays his taxes, and he hasn't left the country. Although there is a warrant out for him, it's impossible to serve it on someone who can't be found."

Bill said, "What about acquaintances? Friends? Who are his friends?"

"Tate says there aren't any, and Hillary agrees," Angus replied. "He's so involved with business that he doesn't have time. He doesn't have the need. He sees the people related to his enterprises, and apparently that satisfies any need for personal contact. There's no family. He's an isolated man. And he pays so well that, when asked, his employees 'don't know' him.''

Bill considered that thoughtfully. "So business is the only thing that holds his attention. Did you find out with whom he deals?"

"His underlings appear to handle it."

Bill could tell he'd been over all this many times. It was only new to Bill.

Angus continued, " 'I'll get back to you' is their favorite expression."

"Women?" Bill asked. "Has he married again?"

"Not that we can discover. But he could have been married out of state. Marriages are state regulated. As for lovers, we can guess, but there's no indication."

Bill pushed up his lower lip and frowned. "What about the Morgan family? Is there any reason we couldn't tap them? The Sawyers are available. While I can vouch for that, I'll make sure. Each family should be fully informed. This isn't something to be lightly undertaken. We all know that. How about the Winklers?" He was referring to another family with extensive connections.

Angus grinned. "So we search for a chink in Dominic's social armor?"

Bill agreed and suggested, "I know of only a couple of people who have their fingers in the Lorenzo pie. There are people who have a wider circle of acquaintances than I. Maybe we can appeal to their humanity."

"It's worth a try. We need someone who has enough security that antagonizing Lorenzo can't rock their own financial boat."

Bill agreed. "We need a humanitarian whose sympathy could lie with a woman whose child has been taken from her, who wouldn't be distracted by deals and who would think of the bereft mother and not just that the child is being cared for and—so what.''

And having settled the next way to approach the problem of Dominic Lorenzo, the two men then began to become acquainted, trading stories and opinions, weighing and judging each other and ending up with the beginnings of a friendship.

Bill arranged for Angus to have lunch with him and representatives from some of the other families who had agreed to help in the search. Again lunch was at his condo. His staff was delighted. They set up round tables and served a perfect meal. The guests ate at leisure, and it was a convivial group. Each was already acquainted with at least a few of the others, and so was Angus.

They were all people whom Bill would tap through friendship or business contacts; people he could trust. Since Angus knew a hell of a lot more than Bill about the situation, it was Angus who presented the case of Dominic Lorenzo to the others. He put all their cards on the table.

Then Bill asked, ''Would any of you or your people be willing to help out? We understand what antagonizing Lorenzo could do to a corporation. There's been some indication of that. So willingness is the primary question. Does anyone in any of your families have any contact with Lorenzo or know of anyone who does?''

One replied, ''Everyone knows of him. I'll have to check to see if any of the family knows of any clubs or spas or whatever. He's so self-contained that he could have a club brought to him—lock, stock and golf course!''

The others smiled, for they already knew that. But the people invited to Bill's were delighted to have been approached for help by two such men of influence. Bill knew they were glad for the contacts and for the clout that could be obtained through acquaintance with the Sawyer family. When those who were there had left, all were committed to the cause of finding Benjamin for Tate.

Angus said to Bill, ''Impressive.''

Bill replied, ''Only if it works.''

''You have one hell of a network.''

''We've been around a long time.''

''You must be honest.'' Angus watched Bill thoughtfully. ''No one else could command that kind of response unless they'd done their share of favors.''

''A lot of them are practically kin—if not in fact, then by osmosis.''

Angus smiled. ''We have connections like that, too.''

And Bill put his hand on Angus's shoulder to say softly, ''I noticed. My thanks for this.''

''It's all in the family. I hope it works.''

Bill nodded.

Tate continued her schedule at the culture center, taping children's books. She, who had given up her child, watched and talked to and held other people's children and read to them. It helped to fill the gap in her life.

She and Bill had been invited to Angus's apartment early one September evening. Because of a taping, Tate was late in getting there, and Bill scolded her,

"You come home drained. Worn-out emotionally. You torture yourself."

"No. It encourages me to believe Benjamin is all right. How could anyone be unkind to a child?"

Angus said, "Lots of people are unkind."

Hillary put her hands into her hair and complained, "Good grief, Angus, did you have to put that in?"

Angus looked surprised. "All I did was answer a question honestly. Tate, you have to know no one is going to harm the son of Dominic Lorenzo."

Tate said, "It's okay. Don't worry about it." But her heart was chilled. Who else had control of her son? What about the others who were in charge of Benjamin?

The talk went on around Tate, and she looked at each speaker and appeared to listen. She was in a strange vacuum for a while. But she gradually shook herself mentally, knowing her worries helped nothing, and rejoined the conversation.

The evening was a leisurely one, but it wasn't very late when Bill said he and Tate had to leave. Tate was a little irked that he was the one to decide they were leaving. She was somewhat parsimonious as they went down the hall to apartment six.

She deliberately delayed in getting ready for bed. She retidied the kitchen, annoyed the stack of neat papers by her computer, needlessly straightening things, then even sat down and picked up her knitting, which she hadn't touched in six months. She had to reread the directions and figure out where she was in the pattern.

Bill watched her with a slight smile. "Are you being independent?"

Quellingly she retorted, "I'm perfectly capable of deciding when I want to go to bed."

"What if I offer to have my naked body there when you get into bed?"

"If you think I'm so tired that I must come home early, then of course I'm much too tired to wrestle around with you."

"Oh, did you want to *wrestle*? I'm not sure I have enough energy for wrestling. I suppose I could manage a couple of falls, but—"

"Oh, be quiet."

"The thrill is gone?" Bill was enjoying himself.

"For now."

"I feel like a used man. One who hangs around, unappreciated, biding the time until you look up and think, 'Oh, so you're here.'"

She raised only her eyes and stared at him.

He was laughing, but then he remembered Tate's having said that Dominic had appeared surprised when he'd found Tate in his bed, as if he'd forgotten until that minute that he was married. Bill could cheerfully have throttled himself.

She looked back at her knitting, but she didn't do anything. Her hands were still.

Bill wondered if he'd hurt her with his careless words. He got up and went to her. He knelt beside her knees and wrapped his arms around her body, then pulled her against him, sliding her forward on the chair. "I'm sorry, Tate. I didn't mean to stir up ugly memories."

"What 'ugly memories'?" she asked vapidly.

"Just now, when I said—"

She interrupted him. "I was coping with the most amazing sweep of desire my body has ever experi-

enced, and I couldn't do anything but try to with-
stand the madness."

He loosened his arms a little and looked at her in
amazement. "What sort of madness?"

"I think my temper has been the result of sexual
withdrawal. You haven't been here in three days, and
I haven't been properly kissed or touched in all that
time. What's so ugly about that memory?"

Bill thought she hadn't remembered being ignored
by Dominic. He adjusted his stance, although still on
his knees. "You need a fix? A quick one? I was just
hoping you wouldn't ravish me tonight. I need some
sweet and tender love. I'm feeling, uh, fragile."

She smiled just a bit. "Are you."

He nodded. Tate could tell he found it difficult to
control his smile. But his hazel eyes sparkled, and he
had to rub his mouth with his big hand. As he knelt
there, his masculine body was so formidable, she
thought that for him to try to be a supplicant was just
ridiculous. He wasn't at all practiced. He was lousy at
trying to look as if he were pleading for tenderness.

"What seems to be the trouble?" she asked with
false solicitousness. "Are you ill?"

He said very earnestly, "I have a fever."

"What sort of fever?" She faked a look of great
concern.

"You've heard of spring fever. I have autumn fever. Any boating man gets it this time of year, when
the weather starts to change and he'll have to take in
his boat and winterize it. This time of year any boat-
man gets autumn fever."

"I don't believe I've ever heard of that."

"Well, having been raised in Texas, where the sun-
shine spends the winter, you don't have to take boats

in from the water. So you might not know about such things. It's my duty to expand your knowledge so you can understand the peoples of the northland.''

"I see. How do you go about 'expanding my knowledge'?''

"Take off your clothes.''

She put her hands to her face and pushed back her hair from her forehead as she stared thoughtfully at the ceiling. "That has such a familiar ring to it. Where have I heard that before?''

"It could be genetic memory. Your people are northwestern Europeans, and they had to cope with the Ice Age when they took in boats each fall.''

"Of course.'' She nodded.

"Ready?''

"I suppose.''

"I'd like a little more enthusiasm there.''

In a normal speaking voice she said, "Rah-rah.''

"I believe it would be better if I helped you. I can see this is your first time. It is absolute hell, dealing with a woman who is untrained in coping with autumn fever.''

She smiled.

"Maybe not,'' he said. "That was a hellcat smile, if ever I saw one.''

"How many hellcats have you known?''

With dismissive impatience he replied, "We aren't working on that. We're working here on recognizing autumn fever.''

"Begin.''

"You can tell it first because of the calendar. If it's this time of year, it's one of the first clues. Then there is a lassitude in the victim.'' She watched as he rose with such lovely ease to stand upright. "A restlessness." He paced about a little. "A pensiveness." He put his hands into his trouser pockets and went over to lean against the side of the window and stare out over the lake.

"I see."

He turned back toward her. "There are physical signs, too."

"Ahh."

"He needs love and understanding. If he's around a woman, she can tell he's needy."

"How?"

He took her hand and pulled her to her feet. "He needs kissing." He showed her how that was. His kiss was consuming, his hands a little rough. He pulled her tightly to him, and his hands went down her back to cup her bottom and pull her closer to him. He lifted his mouth. "Are you beginning to understand?"

She was still reeling from the power of his kiss. She murmured, "My eyes are closed."

"Here." He took her hand and ran it on down his stomach. "Feel?"

"My word. You do have a problem."

"See? You thought it was psychosomatic, didn't you, that autumn fever was all in my imagination?"

"Apparently it's not."

"There's a cure."

She began to laugh.

"You're a good woman. Any woman who is joyful when she hears there's a cure for something as insidious as autumn fever is a woman who helps."

She laughed and wound her arms around his head, to kiss him with all her heart. With her arms up, her body was defenseless, and he took full advantage of the opportunity.

Their kisses were hungry, feeding kisses, and his hands were conquering. But then as he held her he lifted his head and looked at her. Their eyes held in a long, long gaze as they stood there. It was as if they'd moved into another sphere. To another place. Their faces became serious, and their breathlessness wasn't completely sexual.

Their teasing evaporated, and he moved his head slowly down to hers. Their mouths melded; their kiss softened, sweetened. His hands moved differently now, cherishing her. And she was tender as she caressed his head and shoulders.

He lifted her into his arms and carried her to their bed. Their clothing seemed to float away as with no effort they were seemingly instantly naked.

Their bed was a bower; the city sparrows outside the open window became nightingales. The closed linen drapes turned into gossamer, and there had to be a rainbow somewhere. Their mating was magical.

He was awed by the intricate marvel of her body as he worshiped her.

And she knew he was the most beautiful man ever made.

They moved their hands in amazed appreciation of the miracle of each other, and with their lips they sipped and licked and suckled in their efforts to taste.

Their flesh was so sensitized that just the touch of her smooth skin against the texture of his was electrical. And the tiny shock waves of kisses and caresses shimmered like light waves through their bodies.

Tate became somewhat disoriented with so much sensual sensation. Her movements became more languid; her body lax and supple, malleable, and she forgot to breathe.

And Bill became iron hard, sweaty, and his breath was raspy. Every fiber in him was rigid. He bent over her like a predator, and she was his feast. He rubbed his face on her in slow swirls, like a lion marking his property, and his mouth was hot, his body searing, and his breath scalded her.

When he took her, she gasped in ecstasy as she clutched his shoulders. Her lips parted, and she made throaty sounds as her breathing became spasmodic and her body urged his on.

Bill shivered as he fought for control. He closed his eyes, moving his head back. His mouth opened as he groaned. And finding a semblance of momentary control, he bent his head forward to look at the woman under him, his breathing that of a long-distance runner.

Her lashes were on her cheeks, which were flushed with sexual heat. Her lips were parted and vulnerable, her body restless and moving voluptuously, enticing him to completion. She so obviously wanted him that her need was inflaming to him.

He kissed her softly, then rubbed his face around hers. Tate found it exquisitely sexual, that tender claiming, the contrasting feelings of whiskers and flesh on her very susceptible skin. He separated from her and moved his face down her body in those same hot, sweaty, gentle, whiskering swirls—into her throat down to her chest, around each breast, to her stomach, to the apex of her thighs. And he lay back on her again to thrust himself into her as his tongue, too, thrust. He built them to passionate tremors. He took her with him up into yet another world of sensational need, to the zenith, to the crest of that incredible wave, to ride it out.

They lay panting, recovering. Bill had levered his forearms next to her shoulders to take a part of his weight, but his forehead was beside her head, leaning into the pillow. Gradually he realized her broken breathing wasn't just exertion; she was quietly weeping.

He snapped his head up so that he could peer into her face. "Did I hurt you?"

She shook her head.

"What is it?"

"It was just . . . amazing."

"Yes."

"Oh, Bill. Oh, Bill . . ."

"Ah, my love." He slid his hands under her shoulders and controlled their bodies as he turned them, still coupled, until she lay on top of him.

She was like a rag doll that had lost a good deal of its stuffing.

He held her with one arm, and with the other hand he smoothed her hair from the side of her face as she lay there on him, quietly weeping. He was so hot and sweaty that he didn't feel her hot tears on his chest, but his fingers did. He was silent, giving her the comfort she needed with his body and hands. Why was she crying?

When her tears were done, he and Tate lay there still. He felt her left hand go to his side and press gently there, and her right hand smoothed the hair of his chest by her cheek, then it went to his other side and was still. It was a while before he realized that she slept.

Why would she cry? She loved him. A man could tell if a woman only used him or tolerated him. Tate did love him. And that had been a class ten-out-of-ten lovemaking. All sex was good, but this had been re-markable.

Had she had it like that with . . . Lorenzo? Did she grieve for him? Or was it just the boy? For Lorenzo to have snatched the kid and hidden him from Tate showed an emotional revenge that might well cover a frustrated love. Had there been more to their marriage than Tate had indicated?

Even her having said that Dominic had seemed to forget he was married to her could have been a form of punishment. A bid for her to pay more attention to him? What if he were holding Benjamin as bait for Tate to return to him? Why, then, hadn't he made himself available to contact?

Tate was an independent woman. She needed something to occupy herself, her mind, her interest. She was not a toy a man could take home, put on a shelf and only take down occasionally in order to play with it. Inactivity would drive her wild.

Bill's eyes narrowed. Was that what had happened in his own marriage? Had he been guilty of neglect, as Lorenzo had with Tate? But Bill's wife had had affairs while she'd been engaged to him. He hadn't known that until after she'd been pregnant with Jenny. As Lorenzo had briefly doubted Benjamin was his, Bill still questioned whether he was really Jenny's biological father.

Tate was in no way similar to his ex-wife. Tate wasn't a woman who had affairs. And he thought about the desperation that had driven her to the lodge in Canada. His poor Tate. Trapped in an impossible situation. When he and Tate were married he would understand more, and he could be a better husband to her.

But Lorenzo's conduct in this was still very emotional for a man of his business stature. Could he be expecting Tate to come back to him? That would seem strange, since he hadn't contacted her in two years. Perhaps he thought he could drive her to her knees and she'd come back under any terms he dictated.

Bill would never allow that. Any man who could put a woman into such torment, as Lorenzo had Tate, was not balanced. If he could take her child beyond her finding or communication, then he was capable of any torture.

What if Lorenzo was having Tate watched by some of his people? What if he knew exactly what she was doing and all about Hillary's search? What if he was sitting in the middle of his despotic empire like a spider waiting to entice her back into his web? Was Lorenzo dangerous to Tate? What if he found she was having an affair with another man?

More than ever Bill was convinced that he had to find Tate's son for her. His family was as safe as any from possible financial revenge on Lorenzo's part, but Lorenzo still might be able to do them harm.

Bill knew there would be no hesitation from the family in this. He knew that so well, so completely, that he smiled at the ceiling with his regard for them all. They were family oriented.

And he loved Jenny. Whether or not she was really his child in fact, she was still his. And he cared about her. He thought of all the things that had happened to Jenny because he hadn't been paying enough attention. He'd never been faced with anything like his ex-wife, who had no maternal feelings at all. It had never occurred to him that she could be so casually uncaring with a child.

His disgust had been such that he'd had to turn away from the woman. Without even packing Jenny's things, he'd taken her and left. He had only wanted Jenny away from there.

Bill wondered for the first time how Jenny had felt then. How had she seen her father under those circumstances? She must have been confused. This stranger had come in, confronted her mother, taken her away and never said a word. Bill knew that of all that had happened to Jenny, having him for a father hadn't been one of the good things.

But her aunt and uncle had rescued her. They and Beth. Jenny was very fortunate to have them. Bill wondered if he would be doing Jenny any good to take her back, if he and Tate married and began their own family. Or would yet another disruption harm Jenny? It was something they would have to figure out with some professional advice.

He needed to talk to Jenny. He probably never would have realized that if it hadn't been for Tate.

Bill looked at his love lying on his body, replete from his and sound asleep. He was filled with his love for her, this marvelous woman. All his protective, masculine, possessive feelings concentrated on her. He wanted nothing in life so much as her happiness. That would have to include her son. And he searched his problem-solving mind for other avenues that he could use to find the elusive Dominic Lorenzo. And Benjamin.

Nine

——

Bill took Tate to meet the rest of his family. He thought he was clever and handled it well. He told Tate that Jenny wanted to see her grandparents, and would Tate like to go along for the ride?

Tate hadn't been born yesterday. She knew this was the Family Screening. She was a wreck. She asked Hillary, "Whatever shall I *wear*?"

Hillary was trimming Phoebe's claws very carefully, so she replied rather absently, "Clothes."

"Cute. Just the sort of reaction I need right now is for someone I trust, on whose opinion I can rely, to respond with something like that."

Hillary looked up, and commented, "You're a tad touchy."

Tate shrieked.

Hillary watched with interest and observed, "I'm glad Angus's family isn't around here close. We probably won't meet until the wedding at Thanksgiving, and they'll have to accept me and keep their criticism to themselves.''

''You are no help at all!'' Tate accused her hotly.

''Begin as you plan to go on.''

Tate turned from the closet and looked at her baby sister. ''That's really very wise.''

Hillary discounted the wisdom. ''That was first said by Noah's wife.''

''If there wasn't anyone else around then, why did she say that?''

''It was probably when Noah asked if he was expected to clean the bottom of the ark.''

Figuring that out distracted Tate, and she put on whatever Hillary handed her. So she never really knew what she wore the day she met Bill's family—en masse.

Bill thought he'd saved Tate from any stage fright. His family were all avidly curious. Bill's brother Sam had reported that when he'd come home from seeing them at Carol's and casually mentioned that Bill had been there with a woman named Tate, they'd gone wild and questioned eagerly. Sam said they'd rocked him back on his heels, and he'd gotten a headache trying to remember what she'd had on and how she'd looked. ''Nice'' hadn't been at all sufficient.

When Bill and Tate arrived at Princeton, they found that Jenny was giving up a soccer game. Bill couldn't bring himself to drag her away. He called his parents to explain, and was told, Of course! Jenny ran to her room and changed clothes. Bill and Tate drove her to the school grounds, where she threw herself into the battle, running and giving every ounce of energy to the game, which they lost. But the crowd cheered the losers, too; they'd tried so hard.

Bill's pregnant sister and the rest of the family stayed home in Princeton, but Beth went along to the Sawyers'. Beth and Jenny slept all the way to Lincoln.

The Sawyers were very nice to Tate. There were so many of them that she never really sorted out who belonged to whom, but no one seemed to mind, and Bill never left her side. He explained things and events and people, and Tate laughed so much her throat was tired.

And she watched the children. All those beautiful young cousins. Her glances especially followed the youngest ones, those three and four year olds, watching what they did and how they reacted.

And she watched Jenny. Jenny was a little awkward, for she hadn't been down to Lincoln for a while, but she knew all her cousins. Those her age took her in tow, and they trooped in and out, mostly eating and laughing.

Bill managed a meeting of the adult Sawyers, leaving Tate with Jenny and Beth. He told Tate it was family business. At the gathering of his kinspeople, Bill explained exactly how much power Lorenzo possessed, in case the man took revenge. Then Bill explained about Tate's son. In a rather puzzled way, they all agreed to help, asking, Why the questions? Then they smiled and said variations of "Go ahead—we might be able to help through some of the people we know, too."

While that went on, Tate, Jenny and Beth strolled on the Sawyer grounds. "It's beautiful here," Tate remarked.

"It's a home," the girls agreed. And they threw sticks for the two family dogs.

It was a little later when Bill found them, walking along, talking comfortably together, and he was especially conscious of his love for them. "What's going on?" he asked them.

Tate said easily, "We like this place."

Bill looked around. "Dad and Mom really wanted Jenny to come live with them, but here she'd have been an only child."

Jenny said with strong feelings, "I'm glad I'm with Beth. Being the only one your age is really the pits."

Beth smiled at Jenny.

There was an awkward silence then as the two adults were reminded of how long Jenny had been dragged around in her mother's adult world.

To ease the moment, Tate asked, "Those pits. Would they be arm or tar pits?"

Jenny squinted. "I think sweaty arm."

Bill protested, "Now, that's vulgar."

But the other three exchanged a quick, sharing, laughing glance. Tate understood twelve-year-old humor.

Bill saw that, and he was suddenly conscious that there was an easiness developing between the two—his daughter and the woman he loved. He walked between them, wanting to be included in their budding closeness. They bent their heads forward and exchanged a smile across his chest. They shared him.

Because of Jenny's soccer game, their schedule was pushed back all through the day, and Bill and Tate were late in returning Jenny and Beth back to Princeton, which was no big deal. Contented and tired, they'd slept all the way home.

On the way to Chicago the lovers talked over the day. And eventually Tate said casually "Jenny sure looks like all the rest of the Sawyers."

Bill stiffened in surprise. "Do you think so?"

Tate laughed. "How like a man to want to preen over his daughter's looking so like him."

But the idea astonished Bill. "How do you see her as a Sawyer?" He listened intently.

"Bone structure, gestures. Those have to be genetic. She hasn't been around you all enough to have acquired them by mimicry. Her eyes are exactly like yours—the color, the lids, the lashes. How lucky she is to have gotten your lashes."

And Bill was silent as he assimilated the fact that Jenny could well be his.

It was a pleasant drive. The roads were good, the traffic was light at that late hour, and a sax tape was in the deck player.

Bill drove Tate to his place, and she protested, "I'm in slacks. I haven't anything else to wear!"

"Why on earth would you want to wear anything?"

"So it's going to be one of those nights," she guessed.

"Is there another kind?"

"I hope not."

"A hellcat." He smiled smugly. "I've known that since the night I taught you about autumn fever."

"Uh-oh, you're beginning another attack?"

"Yes. It's a little like malaria."

"You've never told me if this is catching. Are you putting me at risk?"

"You don't own a boat yet, do you?" he asked.

"No. Neither do you. You borrowed Angus's."

"No problem. But if you *had* gotten a boat, I have antibodies that would help you deal with any stray bouts of autumn fever."

She gave him a patient look. Then she became aware that the music piped through Bill's condo was...saxophone. She raised her eyebrows. "Anyone else here? It sounds like some dark, smoke-filled dive."

He agreed. "The staff has the weekend off. No one will show up again until Tuesday."

"You will let me go home for fresh clothing?"

"Come see."

He'd bought her a number of outfits—slinky, sexy, scandalous things. She looked at them and laughed until tears ran. He lay on the bed with his head propped on one hand and smiled as he watched her laugh. "Try on the red. I had a heck of a time getting up the nerve to pick it up and buy it. I paid cash and disguised my voice."

She whooped with laughter. But she refused to put on the red thing.

So he plied her with wine. He fed her a snack that his cook had left for them—squares of cheeses and bits of vegetables and all sorts of nibbles. Tate paraded around in the chiffon and feathers and in the heavy pink satin; and she tried on the oversized shirt with the tight-ankled slacks. She even put on the scraps that passed for a swimsuit, but she wouldn't try on the red thing. He gave her some more wine.

"Are you trying to get me inebriated?" she asked.

"You can still pronounce it? What kind of wine is this?"

She took a sip and rolled it around on her tongue and decided, "Kroger's Chablis."

"My God," he breathed in despair.

She raised her eyebrows. "No? I missed? I'll be drummed from the corps in disgrace!"

They drank a toast to Kroger's wine section. She said the glasses were too nice to throw into the fireplace. He agreed. She smiled. "They beat paper cups all hollow."

He laughed.

She wouldn't wear the red thing. But she didn't mind putting the chiffon and feathers back on. She swirled the feathers and dropped the collar down her spine. She flirted. He told her that she wasn't supposed to wear anything under chiffon and feathers, and that did astonish her. "It's completely transparent!"

"Yes."

"That would be shocking."

He grinned. "Shock me."

So she did, but she still wouldn't wear the red thing.

"If you knew what I went through to get that for you, you—"

"For *me*? You're saying you bought that wicked, wicked scrap for me?"

"Who else? *I* certainly can't wear that color. It doesn't go with my eyes."

She peered into his eyes. She frowned and said, "It does match your eyes. They're bloodshot."

"I spent the day driving around all over Illinois," he complained.

"You must be exhausted."

"Almost. Wear it for me. You can close your eyes."

She didn't put it on until Monday at dawn. He looked at her sleepily, depleted, no threat at all, and he just laughed.

She swished and teased, then she put on his hunting boots and carried his duck-walking stick, swinging it. She found his top hat and opened it perfectly to set it on her head. She posed and strutted. She was outrageous.

He laughed, watching her, then he leaped up from the bed with a roar, and she shrieked and ran right out of the boots, flung aside the cane and the hat and made it into the drawing room, but no farther.

On Tuesday Bill had lunch with Angus and the others who were going to help find Dominic and Tate's Benjamin. One said, "No one in our organization or family has any problem with the search. We'll do our damnedest." And they all agreed they could launch the inquiry. They spent the time plotting their course.

So it was begun.

But Bill still didn't mention anything about it to Tate. If it wasn't successful, she might never know how many people had risked their fortunes in trying to help her find Benjamin.

Odd people who Bill had no inkling were involved in the search would report to him about it. Word of his investigation had gradually filtered into unusual places. One of the Sawyer family was searching for a contact with Dominic Lorenzo. The search involved not only Bill but the entire Sawyer family, the Morgan family, and the Behrs.

Bill heard there were questions: "Behrs? Who are the Behrs?"

And the replies were variations of "Who cares? If they're linked with the Sawyers and the Morgans, they must be part of us."

Then the curious asked, "Why would Bill Sawyer want to meet with Lorenzo?"

And the reply closest to accuracy given at first was "He wants a contact. Bill needs to speak with him."

And curiosity became stronger. "Why?" Bill knew they were aware that there was always the faint whiff of a merger or takeover to be ridden profitably.

But the reply wasn't nearly so interesting: "Lorenzo kidnapped his son and hasn't allowed his ex-wife to see him. For two years now."

Bill heard that that had touched a lot of rather callous hearts. Some of the callous ones arranged painful meetings with strangers who were their own children. Some of the meetings even worked, and bonds were formed. All because of Benjamin.

But as word of the search spread, Bill set himself to be patient. He felt there was a good chance of someone's knowing where he could find Lorenzo. And he felt he could reason with the man and arrange for Tate to at least see the boy.

Bill was restless anyway. And it seemed to him that nothing ever happened soon enough. Seemingly fruitless time passed with nothing reported. But he knew the search continued, and the inquiry was spreading even farther. The search had become a game of sorts, like a scavenger hunt. The wives had heard Dominic Lorenzo's name so much that they became interested. And they had access to new places. They began asking around at exclusive boutiques. "Does Dominic Lorenzo pay anyone's bills here?" Bill heard of one inspired wife who asked at the top nanny registry if there was any Lorenzo who was using that service. But there, too, the reply was "Not yet." Such an organization would never just say plain no.

Then Bill had a strange call. A man named Finnig said in almost indecipherably mangled English, "Angus Behr vouches for me; ask him," and hung up.

So what the hell was that about? Bill wondered. He looked at the dead phone, punched the bar for the dial tone and called Angus.

Angus said, "Behr here," in a rather distracted way.

"Hi, this is Bill Sawyer. A man just called who said you would vouch for him. His name is Finnig."

Angus laughed in a roar of humor. "He said I'd *vouch* for him? The *nerve* of that guy."

"You won't?"

"Oh, yes. What's he want?"

Bill replied, "He just said that you'd vouch for him and hung up. I assume he has something to sell—or something to tell?"

"This is a character. Finnig is a very shadowy man. He has wide contacts. When we were searching for Tate, Finnig got involved to the point where my friend Paul pulled his police off the search and left it to Finnig!"

"Who is this man, Finnig?"

"We don't actually know. For helping look for Tate, he asked that I give him the names of clean ships, with good crews. He promised no drugs or illegal shipments. He was offended that I'd clarify that little stipulation."

"What do you suppose he wants?"

"Want me to come along?"

"I'd appreciate it," Bill replied. "Thank you."

"One does as one must for a potential brother-in-law."

"Now how did you figure that out?"

Angus hung up laughing.

Since Bill had no inkling as to why Finnig wanted to see him, he couldn't mention the strange contact to Tate. He'd kept her at his place. But she missed close proximity to her sister, so they moved back to her apartment.

Frustrated with living at her place while his stood empty, Bill told Angus, "Come stay with us at my apartment. There's plenty of room. The house staff needs something to do to justify my paying their wages."

"What about our cat, Phoebe? She can't stay alone here at my place."

"Bring her along. There's pigeons on the balcony."

"Sold."

So they all packed suitcases and moved to Bill's for the next weekend. Being in the luxury apartment with such a competent staff was like being at a resort. There were four bedrooms besides the staff's quarters. There were the living room, parlor/sitting room, the solarium, a study and library and a formal dining room. All had been furnished long ago by Bill's grandfather, who had sold it to Bill in a long, hard haggling that had entertained the entire family and had become funny to Bill only after it was all over.

From that Thursday evening until Monday night, the two couples met for meals that were served in style, and they didn't see one another the rest of the time unless they'd planned an outing together. Phoebe loved the extended adventuring and the fact that the birds felt free to use the balcony, too.

That was when the sisters and Angus began to meet Bill's friends. Angus knew some of them through his contacts in the maritime insurance field. Some names were familiar to him through his family. They were all foreign to Tate and Hillary, whose circle of acquaintances was mostly in Texas.

It was at Bill's that Finnig found them.

Tate asked, "Won't you sit down?"

Finnig replied in words that probably said, "I come to see them." He indicated Angus and Bill.

Then Tate realized the men were waiting for her and Hillary to leave the room. So they did.

Bill said to Finnig, "Sit down. Would you like something to drink? We're having Scotch."

"Believe I will. Who's your liquor dealer?"

After Finnig spoke, there was always a pause while Bill and Angus interpreted his words. Bill replied, "Murray."

"He's a crook. I can get it for you wholesale."

"Really?"

"Yeah. Third the price."

"Real?" Bill was dubious.

"My word."

"Good enough. A case?"

"I make a call." He went to the phone and arranged it—or at least something. He gave Bill's address, then hung up and said, "Tonight."

"Tonight?"

"Yeah."

"Thank you." Bill thought that if Finnig hadn't set up a robbery, then it would really be a case of rotgut

Scotch and he'd just blown a lump of cash. He gave Angus a glance. But Angus was watching Finnig.

Finnig took his drink, sat down and leaned back, taking in the room, breathing as if he could inhale it. He was about Bill's age, maybe a year or so older. He was a plain-looking man, rather anonymous. He was bulky.

Finnig sipped his drink and squinted a little. "It's okay," he said of the liquor, as if he'd made a generous concession.

Bill asked seriously, "You're a connoisseur?"

Finnig agreed, "I know booze."

"What can we do for you, Finnig?" Angus questioned.

"It's what I can do for you. You're looking for a man, right?"

"What man?" Angus asked carefully.

"Dominic Lorenzo." They were the first two words Bill had heard Finnig say clearly.

Bill breathed, "How did you know?"

"Got ways. Why you want him?"

Bill shot a look at Angus, but Angus said, "Tell him."

Finnig lifted his glass slightly to acknowledge that Angus had endorsed him.

So Bill told Finnig all about Tate and Tate's little boy. Finnig listened and sipped his drink. When Bill was finished, Finnig rose, placed his glass on a table with an inlaid top and shook hands with both men. "I'll see what I can do. The case of Scotch is on the house. If you like it, you can buy the next."

"Thank you," Bill said.

Finnig lifted a hand negligently and left.

Bill took out his handkerchief, lifted Finnig's glass from the wooden table and carefully wiped the ring of moisture from the inlaid wood. Seeing that Angus watched, Bill explained, "It came from England in 1625. If this glass had left a water mark, my housekeeper would have had my hide."

"I have a mother who's like that."

The case of Scotch was delivered about five minutes later. Bill was surprised, but Angus said with a kind of fatalistic acceptance, "He probably had it in his car. More than likely he knows what kind of underwear you wear."

"What do you think about his looking for Lorenzo?"

"It can't hurt. He has connections you wouldn't believe."

"Don't tell Hillary."

"Right," Angus agreed. "We'll say Finnig was peddling booze."

"Shall we try some?"

"I promise you it's the real stuff and legit. I'd bank on it."

"Amazing."

With a smoky character like Finnig, Bill halfway expected to have his place robbed, since Finnig had the address and he'd looked the place over with some care. He said as much to Angus.

Angus explained, "You're probably on his guard list. Hillary and I are followed by his men whenever we go out. They seem to know where we're going before we do. The apartment is probably bugged." He added grudgingly, "I've looked."

"Why would he guard you . . . and now us?"

"It's a strange world. I have no idea. He inadvertently got in on Tate's disappearance, then two of his men panicked when they were delivering Hillary and me to where Tate was to be released. I think that embarrassed Finnig. At least one of the men is still alive. So his discipline couldn't have been fatal. Finnig may well have gone legit."

"Gone . . . legit?"

"He has long fingers in this town. Fingers that aren't acquired in the usual way. He has a lot of clout for a man so young. He has to be only about . . . oh . . . between thirty-five and forty."

"Who took Tate? Was it Lorenzo?"

"No."

"Then who?" Bill asked with a frown.

"They have no idea."

"But you do?"

"There are always speculations," Angus replied vaguely. But that was as far as he would go.

That night when Bill made love to Tate and he had her almost drugged with her desire for him, he coaxed her in a deep, passionate whisper, "Let me give you babies." He was very emotional about it. He felt so sorry about her having lost Benjamin. If he couldn't find Benjamin for her, maybe other babies would ease her grief.

Tate became still. She opened her eyes, her passion suspended. Bill's babies? But he said only for her to allow him to father them. Nothing about marriage.

She could handle being a single mother. She knew Bill would be involved; he would visit. She had a good income. No one else would have to support her. She could do it.

Her parents wouldn't approve. They'd worry for the child. It wasn't fair to the child, to selfishly make such a decision for it. She looked up at Bill and parted her lips to take a breath in order to reply—

When he said, "We could be married in Texas at Thanksgiving, with Hillary and Angus. A double wedding. Two for the price of one. That should please your hard-nosed dad. Fredericka is still there. Roberta and Georgina could come in for the celebration. We could trigger a family reunion. My clan would all go down. Could Jenny be a bridesmaid? How about Beth?"

"Uh . . . well . . . yes."

"The whole package? Marriage, Texas, Jenny, babies . . . and me?"

"Oh, Bill. Yes. The whole package."

He moved from her side and left the bed. He went to his dresser and returned with a token ring. "This is just so I had something to put on your finger now. It's only a couple of carats. I'd like to've gotten you one with at least twenty-four, but your gloves would never fit over it."

She was appalled. "*Twenty-four carats?* That would be too big. Good heavens, Bill, anyone who would wear a ring with twenty-four carats could afford to walk in an atmospheric bubble with temperature control and not *have* to wear gloves!"

It was a single, perfect stone. Sitting naked on the bed, her legs curled to one side, Tate held up her left hand to look at the ring. "It's beautiful."

"You are my love."

"It's too big. Let's trade it for something a little less gaudy."

"Gaudy?" Bill, a Sawyer, tasted the unknown word.

"It's too big. See? It doesn't stay centered; it slips around sideways."

He dismissed the inconvenience. "It only needs to be fitted."

"I'd have to keep my fingers closed so it wouldn't go all the way around under my palm. I wouldn't be able to do anything, wearing a ring like that. Did you buy this for Kimberly?"

"What?"

She narrowed her eyes and asked, "Why do you have an engagement ring? Did you buy it in Canada and go back to give it to her when you broke your leg?"

"Don't be ridiculous."

"Ridiculous? Because I don't want to be second choice?"

"Honey, look, I'm thirty-eight years old. I would have to've been interested in one or two women by this time, or I wouldn't be normal."

She gave him a slow look. "I believe you're normal."

"You noticed?" He moved closer.

"Here and there," she admitted, adjusting her body to his closeness.

His voice was gravelly. "Where . . . exactly?"

She put her finger on his mouth, and he kissed her. She indicated his hands next, and he put them on her. She then showed him other indications of interest, and he proved she was right.

Having decided on the double ceremony at Thanksgiving, Hillary and Tate got together at Tate's apartment and called their parents to ask permission. Since theirs was such chatty family who all wanted to talk at once, they had speaker phones. Tate warned her parents, "There are a lot of Sawyers. Where will we put them?"

Her unflappable mother said, "Your father will think of something."

The daughters exchanged laughing glances. That was what their mother always said, and then everyone gave her credit for the solution. Their papa didn't mind at all.

Hillary said the Behr family wasn't as sprawling as the Sawyers and Lamberts. Angus had told her that they were calm and tidy.

Mr. Lambert said that would be refreshing.

Then Hillary asked, "We haven't decided what to wear. Any suggestions? Shall we be formal or casual? Would the church be available at Thanksgiving?"

And Mrs. Lambert replied, "Let's have it here, at home. There are all those family wedding dresses stored in the attic. Let's use those. We have that great central staircase, and we'll set up an altar near the solarium. I married your father just to have that staircase for our daughters. You all know that. Without that staircase as an inspiration, we'd have had all sons. So it's only right to use the stairway."

The daughters saw the logic of that.

Word spread through their Chicago friends and the couples threw their own engagement party at Bill's, which gave the staff something to do. It was beautifully done, and there was an interesting variety of people who mixed well.

Tate began to get the feeling she was being absorbed by Bill and a different life, and she wasn't quite ready to relinquish her past. Her past was really only her small, lost son. She couldn't quite give him up. Or maybe it was only hope that wouldn't quit.

Bill saw that hope and worked on it. He would look at Tate and remember how when he first met her he'd felt his life was through. And he looked at his life now—with Tate: it was beginning again.

Ten

___

Behrs, Sawyers and Lamberts came for the double wedding that Thanksgiving down in Texas. To accommodate the overflow, the Lamberts rented nine house trailers, which they parked among the trees nearby.

A generator was set up to supply the trailers, and catering was arranged for their meals, but everyone still had to work, there were so many people.

It was a marvelous time. Everyone had sore throats—from the children, who yelled *constantly*, to the adults, from laughter.

It was only then that Bill began to understand the wealth the modest Lamberts disregarded.

Bill mentioned to Tate, "It's a good thing the clans are friendly. They could really cause a donnybrook here, like this. My groomsmen could beat the tar out of yours." He smiled, having thrown down the gauntlet.

She gave him a lofty, quelling look. "Behrs and Lamberts go together. If it weren't for our parents, I'd challenge you and just see about that."

"Baseball? And I get Jenny." He lifted his eyebrows, snidely smug.

"That's not fair," Tate protested.

They purposely spoke so that Jenny heard, and she was pleased.

They split the Behr family between them, and when the game was completed, Bill gave a dirty laugh that his side had won. The Lamberts said that was purely rude of him—especially since the Lamberts had *allowed* the Sawyers to win because they were guests.

That got Yankee hoots.

The families got along remarkably well. With some respect, Bill's father said to Tate's father, "Yours is a well-known name in Texas."

But Mr. Lambert discounted there being any honor in that. "It's just that we've *been* here so long. We started out growing cotton, we go back such a long time. Then when cattle was the cash crop, we damned near had to change our name, it having *lamb* in it that way and all. There's just something about the word *lamb* that sets cattlemen's teeth on edge.

"One of our boys, back a ways, almost couldn't marry the girl of a cattleman, just because her daddy took exception to our name! But the gal had hysterics and brought her daddy around. The only thing that saved the name, intact, was we found oil. An oil-coated 'lamb' is surprisingly acceptable."

Everyone easily agreed about that.

Bill and Tate didn't actually "see" anyone else. Their rather vapid gazes clung to each other, their hands touched, they found corners where they could kiss lingeringly. But someone always turned up. The adults said "Here, here! None of that!" while they laughed with glee. And the kids shouted "They're at it again!" and danced around the pair, who had no privacy at all.

Bill waited until Tate was swooning with desire before he asked, "No second thoughts? This is forever, you realize."

"How can you know that when we've both had failed marriages?"

"This is different."

She smiled nicely.

She now wore a slightly smaller diamond on the fourth finger of her left hand. She thought it was beautiful. But he'd had the two-carat diamond set into a drop that included two other diamonds of equal size. An intricately lovely chain allowed Tate to wear it around her throat. "You can call that other one your engagement ring, but this one committed you to me."

All of Tate's sisters were there. Fredericka was still home "between jobs" as she waited for Sling to realize he couldn't live without her and that she was interested in him.

Georgina came in from California and Roberta from D.C. The five sisters, Jenny and Beth went to the attic with the mothers-in-law and various aunts and cousins. There they searched through the trunks, looking for things to wear for the ceremony. As each gown was taken from its blue paper wrappings, they found it was labeled by a comment: "Cousin Matilda wore that when..." or "Your Great-Aunt Fanny had

that made up when..." And family history was re-
freshed.

Tate's gown had been purchased long, long ago by
an ancestress in Paris. It was of Egyptian cotton and
was encrusted in pearls. Pearls hung dangling from the
short sleeves, from around the ankle-length hem and
from around the scooped neckline.

Each of the others found a gown that pleased her.

Portions of the Lambert yard were filled with
hedges of poinsettias that were just beginning to
bloom, and there were all sorts of mums. The family
had the two-story solarium filled with potted flowers,
and even put different pots of grasses in the adjoining
screened birdcage, which was also two stories high. It
held five canaries, which sang their hearts out...
echoed note by note by the wild mockingbirds.

The Lamberts were used to entertaining crowds, and
Thanksgiving was a sit-down dinner. Drop-leaf tables
holding all their expanding leaves were set around to
form one long table that snaked through the double-
doored, lower rooms. Tablecloths overlapped, and
several sets of sterling flatware and fragile china were
used. Not all the chairs matched. Children were mixed
in with the adults. There were fifteen people to serve
the platters and bowls of the traditional Thanksgiving meal, and they were busy. And through it all, there
was endless talk and much laughter.

The marriages were to take place Saturday. On Friday all the fragile but surprisingly sturdy antique
dresses were washed by hand and hung on the line to
dry in the light November breeze.

To her daughters Mrs. Lambert said of the fragile
gowns, "Quit worrying. They'll do fine."

On that day Finnig arrived at the Lambert house and asked to speak to Bill Sawyer. The elderly man who was the Lambert doorman invited the stranger inside to wait. And Finnig trod into the Lambert house with interest. It was then that he saw Georgina.

Georgina was thirty-one. She was blond, and like the rest of the Lambert daughters she was tall, slender and blue eyed. She came through the downstairs room as their doorman admitted Finnig.

The doorman explained, "He come to see Tate's man." He took Finnig's coat—which he'd carried over his arm—and hung it in the cavernous closet under the staircase.

Georgina smiled and came over to Finnig, the unexpected guest. "You're a friend of Bill's? He's around somewhere. I'm Tate's sister, George. Actually, it's Georgina."

Finnig breathed, "Georgina."

"Won't you sit down? Bill and Tate sneak off a lot. No one leaves them a minute to be alone. Are you from Chicago?"

Finnig nodded.

"How nice you could come down for the wedding. Here, sit here. May I offer you something cooling? This is typical Texas winter weather, just as we advertise."

"It's nice," he said clearly.

"Have you ever been to Texas before?"

"No."

With an expression of great curiosity and with some caution, Bill came into the room. He gave a quick look to be sure George wasn't shocked, and saw that she would handle anyone with ease and that Finnig hadn't said anything wrong—yet. "Well, hello. What a surprise." All true. What the hell was Finnig doing there? Unless—

He turned to George. "Would you excuse us?"

"Surely." She rose, then turned and said, "You'll stay for lunch? Do." She smiled before she left the room, not waiting for Finnig to reply.

Finnig had risen as Georgina departed, and he now stood, entranced, as he stared after her.

Bill asked, "Do you have news of Benjamin?"

Finnig brought his stare to Bill, focused with some effort and was a little surprised to find Bill in front of him. "What?"

Bill found it so interesting to hear Finnig put a *t* sound to that word that Bill took a second to acknowledge the fact. He said, "Do you have some word for me? What are you doing here?"

Finnig reached into his pocket, took out an envelope and handed it to Bill. Bill looked at him and frowned, then opened it and took out two pictures. They were of a little boy. In one shot he was walking to a car, and in the other he was climbing the stairs of a public building. He was with adult male legs both times. The adult bodies were cut off, so only the child was in the pictures. Bill asked softly, "Benjamin?"

"Yes."

Bill noted Finnig had said the full word.

"On my honor."

That caused Bill to blink. "Where is he?"

"In Chicago."

"Visiting?"

"They live in Winnetka."

"My God." Finnig, of all people, had found Dominic? "How did you find him . . . them?"

"I got—have connections."

Bill stared carefully at the pictures as he listened to Finnig's enunciated words.

"Lorenzo is married. His wife will have a baby soon."

Bill was astonished to hear Finnig speak in a bland, normal Midwestern accent. He glanced at the man. Finnig even looked different. "Can we see Dominic?"

"Not yet. The pictures are a wedding present. Give them to her at the right time. She'll cry."

Bill said, "Yes." Pictures of Benjamin. How could he just . . . give them to Tate? When? He lifted his glance to Finnig's. "I owe you."

"No. This is friendship."

Bill put out his hand. "Then, thank you."

Finnig turned to leave, but just then Georgina came back with Hillary and Angus. They were followed by Bill's brother Sam, and Tate's father. Angus acted cautious, and Hillary was surprised and exclaimed, "Why, Finnig! What are you doing here? You're just in time for the wedding!"

Finnig flushed and began to shake his head, and George said, "He's staying for lunch."

Finnig looked as if he'd been thrown into water and couldn't swim.

Sam asked, "What's going on?"

Bill replied smoothly, "This is an associate. He brought me some vital information. And he's just lea—"

But Sam held out his hand and said, "I'm Sam Sawyer."

Finnig grasped the hand and replied, "I'm Quintus Finnig."

"Quintus!" exclaimed Hillary. "What a good name. Daddy, this is an acquaintance from Chicago. My father, Jaff Lambert."

As the two men shook hands, Hillary exchanged a laughing glance with Angus.

Bill saw that and knew Hillary would carry the farce right on through. He shook his head a little at Angus, and Angus shrugged minutely.

But Quintus Finnig said to Sam, and to Georgina's father, "How do you do?"

That put blank expressions on several faces.

Although he sweat, Quintus replied in full words and with courtesy. The hosts easily included him. He never got the chance to escape, and Angus's and Bill's efforts to extricate him from the Lambert/Sawyer/Behr entrapment of hospitality were futile.

Worse, Georgina made herself the hostess of this stranger in the crowd, who spoke so slowly and so briefly.

Quintus was asked what he did, and he replied that he had several businesses. Bill and Angus exchanged some interested looks, and Hillary and Tate also shared quite a few amazed glances.

And the rest of the families absorbed Quintus into their midst without really noticing. Bill and Tate found it rather entertaining.

Quintus not only stayed for lunch but was there for dinner as well. Then one of the neighbors found a bedroom at his place for Bill's friend. So Finnig was at the wedding.

As the sisters and Jenny and Beth all dressed for the occasion in the Lambert family finery, there were several giggling whispers between Tate and Hillary over the unexpected witness. And they wondered how and why he'd shown up. They had questioned Angus and Bill, who said Finnig had been making some inquiries for them.

The most amazing thing was Quintus's newly revealed ability to speak clearly.

Actually, he fit in perfectly. He caught the Texas poor-boy trait of lousing up grammar on occasion, so his lapses were accepted as if he'd been deliberate.

Just before the marriages, while the various brothers helped the bridegrooms ready themselves, Angus and Bill were teased: "Do you need any advice for tonight?"

In the laughter and commenting, Angus found time to ask Bill, "Why is he here?"

So Bill showed Angus the pictures.

But Angus said, "How do we know that's Benjamin?"

"On Finnig's honor."

Angus could only stare.

Then Bill cautioned Angus, "I'll be leaving first. It'll be up to you to mind the fox."

"Right."

Jenny and Beth were first down the grand staircase. They were sparkling eyed and pretty in high-waisted lawn gowns of pale floral patterns. The five sisters were in various picture-book gowns and came down as if they had been playing dress-up and were suddenly serious as they joined the adults.

All eyes were on the stairs to see the lovely bouquet of young women descending.

Bill's stare never left Tate. She was beautiful. She was his. For all the rest of her life—and his—they were one. She was exquisite. And she belonged to him. She would be Mrs. William Tremaine Sawyer.

The ceremony was the known one. The replies were firm. The two couples looked at each other, knowing what they pledged, and their hearts were given fully. Their kisses of commitment were gentle.

Then the whole house seemed to erupt into celebration.

Since there was no way that Tate, in that pearl-encrusted gown, could sit down, the dinner had been planned as a buffet, with the children to be served in the solarium. Then, later, the rugs were rolled away for dancing.

Quite seriously, Finnig danced with all the ladies. He partnered them all in turn, from the mothers of the brides and grooms to the littlest girls. He didn't say much. But he danced with Georgina—all the slow ones.

As the Sawyer newlyweds made their thank-yous and goodbyes, Bill and Angus exchanged another meaningful look, of question and assurance, over the "fox" in the Lambert "henhouse." Then Bill and Tate were off in a shower of rose petals.

They drove down to San Antonio to spend the night there. They would then continue on to Padre Island. Tate asked, "Why the suite? We're both so tired we'll probably act briefly like rabbits, then sleep like logs."

They were standing in the middle of their bedroom, still dressed. He took her into his arms and hugged her gently. Now was the time. "I wanted you to have the feeling of space. We've been a little crowded, with all the families there. It was a beautiful time. All of it. Thank you for marrying me."

"You're welcome. And thank you. I love being your wife. I believe it's because I love you quite a bit."

"That much, do you?"

"Oh, Bill."

They embraced. It wasn't just hugs and kisses; it was more formal, more committed, than that. More emotional. It was an embrace. Tate sighed and laid her head on Bill's chest.

He told her, "Your gown was lovely, and on you it was magic."

"Isn't it strange to remember all those who've come before you? All the people who've had children and cared for them so that you can be here now. I'm glad all your people survived."

"I'd have found you through one family or another."

"Oh, Bill."

That time they kissed. He waited. "Tate—"

"Why did Finnig come down to see you? Wasn't it a surprise? How did he find you? Did you tell him we were going to be married?"

"Finnig volunteered to do a search for me."

"Something in particular? For him to come clear down here to Texas, and for him to be able to speak! He's astonishing. I think he's going legit."

"He brought something for you."

"A wedding gift?"

"In a way. I don't know when to give it to you, Tate. I'm so anxious for you to have it that my judgment isn't very good. But I don't want you to wait."

"What in the world?"

"We've been searching for Benjamin."

"Oh, Bill..." Her eyes widened, and her voice became a whisper.

"Finnig believes he's found Lorenzo. And Tate, on his honor he says these are pictures of Benjamin taken last week. Here. Sit down. Tate? Are you okay?"

She hurried to sit down as she bobbed her head and held out her hands, her lips parted, her whole body *intense*.

He gave her the two pictures and turned on a light by her chair. She held the two photographs as if they would crumble. She didn't breathe. He squatted beside her. "Breathe, Tate. Tate!" Her eyes were enormous, and the pupils were dilated almost to the rims of her irises. She scared him a little. "Honey?"

"I'm okay." But she shivered.

He was unnerved. What had he done?

Very gently she began to weep. Tears spilled over. Trembling, she put the photos side by side on the edge of the table. Then she clasped her hands together and stared at the pictures, weeping. Her lips formed the word "Benjamin."

"Tate. Look at me."

She was in something like shock. But her eyes focused on Bill, then she looked again at the pictures. He was four. His hair black. In one picture his eyes were on the camera in the dismissive way of children. In the other he was looking ahead, ready to enter the car.

"It's he?" Her voice was unsteady.

"On Finnig's honor."

"May we fly to Chicago now?"

"The time will come when you will see him. Ah, Tate, have I thrown you into a spin? Should I have waited?"

"No. No, no, no, no, no! I love you! How did you find him? Isn't he beautiful? He looks well, don't you think? Look at his face. My baby. Oh, Bill! What a lovely wedding gift!''

"One of the ironies of all time is that the Sawyers, the Behrs and all the extensions of all our families have put out word all over the world, searching for Lorenzo. Think of all the business connections in this world. I doubt we missed one. Everyone was looking for Lorenzo. And *Finnig* comes to me, that night he gave us the Scotch—do you recall?'' She nodded. "And *he*'d heard I was looking for Lorenzo. Now, how had he ever heard that? And of all those connections, all over everywhere, it was Finnig—in Chicago—who found Benjamin. And he brought the pictures to you as a wedding gift.''

"You began this search? Oh, Bill, how can I thank you?''

"Honey, I wasn't the one who found Benjamin. It was Finnig.''

"It was you who began the search. Without that, Finnig wouldn't have heard.''

"You're welcome, Tate. I would do anything for you.''

They kissed, long and lovingly. He took off her clothes and pulled a satin gown on over her head. He called room service for some warm milk with a little vanilla and some sugar cookies. Then he tucked Tate into bed. When room service promptly delivered the milk and cookies, Bill tipped the boy and locked the door. Then he went to Tate, placed the tray within reach and ordered her to drink it all.

She was silent, nibbling the cookies, watching him undress. She sipped the milk. And she began to become animated. She got up and fetched the pictures, turning on the bedside-table light. She peered at the pictures, smiling at them, teary eyed.

"Isn't he beautiful? Look how straight he stands. That confident turn of his head. They must treat him well. See? His head's up. He doesn't cling. He walks alone. With attention. What a male look he gave the camera. Was that a zoom lens?"

"I believe so, from the print. He's a great-looking boy, Tate. Tell me that I did right in giving you the pictures tonight."

"Oh, yes. Oh, my love. I *love* it that you couldn't wait." She put the pictures aside and got up to walk across the unsteady springy bed. "I love you that you didn't. How kind you are to me!" She flung herself off the bed, and he caught her.

She wrapped her arms around his neck and kissed him long and hard. He kissed her back and smiled down at her. "Go drink your milk."

"Yes, sir."

He patted her bottom as she climbed back up onto the wide bed and walked back across it to sit down, cross-legged, and pick up the pictures yet again.

"Drink your milk."

She absently reached, took a quick peek to check, picked up the glass and sipped.

"Are all the cookies gone?" he asked.

"You may have one."

"I'm impressed. You didn't eat anything for supper."

"I was holding in my stomach and trying to make my bosom smaller. The gown was stretched to its limits. One seam popped. That whatever-great-grandmothers was about six inches shorter than I. And narrower."

"I'm glad you're six inches taller and wider."

"You could choose a better word than 'wider,' for Pete's sake," she chided him.

"Give me a sip of your milk?"

"Why didn't you get your own?"

"You make it look as if it tastes good."

She took a token sip and handed him the glass. "We'll have to have the pictures of Benjamin copied for the family. For my parents and grandparents, especially. They've missed him so badly. I wonder if our children will resemble Benjamin, if there will be a family mark. He doesn't look at all like Dominic."

That was some comfort to Bill. "How many children are we going to have?"

"Three. There's time for three. What do you think?"

"Six."

She turned and gave him a quelling glance. "Six? That sounds like a man who has all the fun and lets someone else do all the work."

"I'd be glad to help out in any way I can."

"How generous of you." She picked up the pictures again. "Do you think it will be possible to actually see him? I know I said if only I could see a picture of him, and I love it that you've made this possible, but do you think . . . ?"

"We're going to try our damnedest."

She smiled over at Bill, her eyes swimming in tears. "Oh, Bill." She went on smiling, then her smile faded away and she said, "This is our *wedding* night."

"I know that, Mrs. Sawyer."

"Did I tell you that you looked so handsome when I came down the stairs? I was almost breathless, because you love me enough to marry me. I would have been willing to be your mistress if you had wanted only that."

"How come you're mentioning that only now?"

"It seemed wisest not to say anything earlier."

"Oh, Tate. Come over here."

It was just before Christmas when Bill finally met with Dominic Lorenzo. Bill went to an office not far from his own, as Finnig had arranged. The new snow was clean, and the holiday air was over all of the city. The Salvation Army officers rang the bells on street corners, and the cold wind hurried people along.

When the secretary courteously escorted Bill to Lorenzo's office, Dominic rose from his desk and stood with equal courtesy. Bill said, "I understand congratulations are in order. Your wife and new son are doing well?"

"Yes. Thank you. Sit down. Please." The "please" was tacked on; it sounded like an unusual word on Dominic's tongue.

Bill sat and waited. Finnig had set this up. The amazing Finnig. How? Would Bill ever know?

Dominic said, "I am hearing that you searched for me. I hear it from all quarters. Was it only for the boy?"

Bill nodded. "Tate's boy."

"And mine."

Bill was silent, thinking it wisest not to push.

"Tate has custody of Benjamin. I did wrong in taking him. Fiona has made me promise to give him back to Tate. Do you want him?" He turned and seemed to assess Bill's reaction.

Surprised, Bill smiled. He stood up and reached to shake hands with Dominic. "Quite frankly you had me over a barrel. You could have demanded almost anything of me."

"Ah," said Dominic. "I wish I'd known." Then he added pensively, "I shall miss the boy."

"I'm sure Tate will be generous about giving you time with Benjamin." He couldn't resist adding, "She will know how you want to see him."

"Tell her I am sorry. I hadn't thought she would grieve so for him. Finnig told me."

"How do you know Finnig?"

"By surprise." Dominic smiled. "An interesting character. I can find nothing wrong with his operations."

"Nor can we. When may Tate see Benjamin? When can we have him?"

"I find this very hard. He is such a nice little boy. I'm very proud of him."

"These kinds of things are very tough. I have a daughter—"

"Finnig told me about that. I know of your ex-wife."

Bill didn't reply. There was nothing to say.

"Well—" Dominic seemed awkward "—I don't quite know what else to say. Will you contact me? To tell me if I can see Benjamin? Could he visit us sometime? My wife has become very attached to him. That's why her heart was so soft for Tate, and she worried about her. Then she learned how Tate grieved... Yes," he said, acknowledging that Tate's grief had touched him.

"I'll ask Tate," Bill promised.

"Thank you."

"You've done the right thing. I believe I can guess what this has cost you."

"Yes. Here is my address." Dominic handed Bill a card. "I might suggest you visit several times and have him visit you before we move him to your place. I'm not sure anyone knows exactly how to do this to a child. He cried for his mother for a long time after I took him." Dominic stood with his head down.

Watching him, Bill understood Dominic was not quite the ruthless man Tate thought him to be.

Bill drove Tate to see Benjamin that afternoon. She carried no gifts. She was a nervous wreck. "He won't remember me." She said in agitation, "Oh, Bill." She asked, "What shall I say?" She wrung her hands as she repeated helplessly, "Oh, Bill..."

"How can you ask me what to say when I took you along to help me with a twelve-year-old? You'll do great. He's your little boy. See if you can remember what you shared. How did you talk to him then?"

At Dominic's house the door was answered not by the maid but by Fiona. She smiled and said, "At last."

Tate hugged her. "Finnig told me how hard you tried to help me."

Fiona's laugh was filled with sympathy. "That Finnig, he does try to save the world. I'm glad he helped you. Benjamin is a dear child."

"Where...?" Tate couldn't think of a way to ask.

Fiona smiled kindly. "This way."

Bill asked Tate, "Would it be better if I waited here?"

"No, come with me."

Fiona took Tate's hand as if she were younger and needed leading. She did. They went down a hall to a door, and Fiona tapped on the panel.

A little voice called, "Come in."

Fiona opened the door, and Benjamin turned around from his cars on the floor. Seeing guests, he stood up to say "Hello."

It was obvious he had been not only well cared for but trained well. Fiona said, "This is your mama."

Alone, Tate walked several steps into the room and sank to her knees as Benjamin watched with interest.

He said, "No. Mama here." He went to a tape player, took a tape, put it into the child's machine and punched a button. Tate's voice came out! It was a copy of one of the library tapes.

She couldn't speak.

Benjamin explained the voice: "Mama."

Tate told her son, "That is I. Listen to my voice. I read that book to you."

He didn't quite believe her.

She opened her purse, and took out a little book and held it out to him. "I used to read this to you."

"My book! That's my book." He came to her and took the well-used little book into his hands. "Mine!" He grinned and hugged the book. "Read to me." And he sat down on her knees as if he'd done it just that morning, and leaned his head back on her breast. The sight undid the three adults. Tears blinded Tate. Tears of joy. Her entire body reacted to that little body on her lap, and she was filled with maternal love. It had been so long. She slid one arm around his sturdy body, and her heart was filled to overflowing. And the two adults who watched were similarly affected.

Fortunately Tate knew the words by heart. She "read" them, turning the pages at the correct times, and Benjamin said, "Good book."

Nothing is easy. They knew that. Nor are such things simply done. There would be tense times and tears and frustration, but it would work out. No growing or changing was ever smooth. But for then, all was well. Tate turned her tear-blinded eyes back over her shoulder and smiled at Bill, reached out her hand to him and brought him down by them so that she could introduce him to her son. Now his son, too.

They were a family of four. And with a fascinated and entertained Jenny, it was a merry Christmas.

The parents watched Jenny laugh as Benjamin stacked the empty gift boxes in the litter of the aftermath of gift giving. Tate and Bill smiled at each other, and they knew they had the greatest gifts God could give.

And before the next Christmas there would be one more.

* * * * *

There are still more Lambert sisters!
Look for Lass Small's books in
Silhouette Desire.

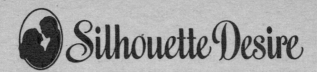 **Silhouette Desire**

If you liked Lass Small's **Hide and Seek** (Desire #453), you'll want to read more about the Lambert sisters in:

Blindman's Bluff (Desire #413)
Kimberly and Logan have to spend two weeks together in order to split a sizable legacy. They're both gung ho about it—until they get a look at each other!

Goldilocks and the Behr (Desire #437)
Angus Behr finds Tate's little sister Hillary in his bed. He roars about it some, but then he just can't let her go, for this she-Behr is just right!

TALES OF THE RISING MOON
A Desire trilogy by Joyce Thies

MOON OF THE RAVEN—June (#432)
Conlan Fox was part American Indian and as tough as the Montana land he rode, but it took fragile yet strong-willed Kerry Armstrong to make his dreams come true.

REACH FOR THE MOON—August (#444)
It would take a heart of stone for Steven Armstrong to evict the woman and children living on his land. But when Steven saw Samantha, eviction was the last thing on his mind!

GYPSY MOON—October (#456)
Robert Armstrong met Serena when he returned to his ancestral estate in Connecticut. Their fiery temperaments clashed from the start, but despite himself, Rob was falling under the Gypsy's spell.

ATTRACTIVE, SPACE SAVING BOOK RACK

Display your most prized novels on this handsome and sturdy book rack. The hand-rubbed walnut finish will blend into your library decor with quiet elegance, providing a practical organizer for your favorite hard-or soft-covered books.

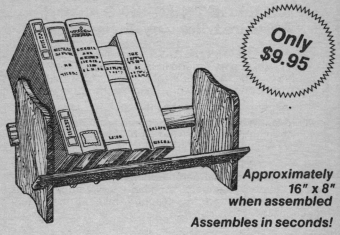

Only $9.95

Approximately 16" x 8" when assembled

Assembles in seconds!

To order, rush your name, address and zip code, along with a check or money order for $10.70* ($9.95 plus 75¢ postage and handling) payable to *Silhouette Books.*

Silhouette Books
Book Rack Offer
901 Fuhrmann Blvd.
P.O. Box 1396
Buffalo, NY 14269-1396

Offer not available in Canada.

*New York and Iowa residents add appropriate sales tax.

BKR-2A

In October
Silhouette Special Edition
becomes
more special than ever
as it premieres
its sophisticated new cover!

Look for six soul-satisfying novels
every month . . . from
Silhouette Special Edition

 *Silhouette Desire*

COMING NEXT MONTH

#457 NIGHT CHILD—Ann Major
Part of the **Children of Destiny** trilogy. Years ago Julia Jackson had been kidnapped before young Kirk MacKay's eyes. Now an amazing turn of events offered him a second chance....

#458 CALL IT FATE—Christine Rimmer
Wealthy Reese Falconer had spurned Cassie Alden's awkward teenage advances. But when a twist of fate brought them together, he could finally take what he'd really wanted nine years before.

#459 NO HOLDS BARRED—Marley Morgan
The long-awaited prequel to *Just Joe*. When Cole Baron rescued an inebriated Jassy Creig from the honky-tonk bar, he knew there was one man she'd never be safe from—him!

#460 CHANTILLY LACE—Sally Goldenbaum
When Paul Forest investigated the mysterious pounding in his grandmother's attic, he didn't know which was more surprising—finding beautiful, dusty Rosie Hendricks . . . or his irresistible urge to kiss her.

#461 HIT MAN—Nancy Martin
Maggie Kincaid didn't trust Mick Spiderelli's fallen angel looks or hit man reputation, but her daughter was in danger. Soon taking care of the Kincaid women became Mick's particular specialty.

#462 DARK FIRE—Elizabeth Lowell
Cynthia McCall was thoroughly disillusioned with men *and* their motives until she met Trace Rawlings. The handsome guide was more man than she'd ever known—but could she trust her heart?
